G000146133

HERE TOMORROW
GONE TODAY

A sparkling collection of stories from the
inventive young writer, Tim Kennemore.
Some are school stories, bringing a fresh
new slant to those perennial school problems such as bullying prefects and class
cheats. The others are set in the future
and offer a hilariously ghastly glimpse into
what may be in store for us all.

TIM KENNEMORE

Here Tomorrow, Gone Today

A Magnet Book

First published in 1983 by Faber and Faber Ltd
This Magnet edition published 1984
by Methuen Children's Books Ltd
11 New Fetter Lane, London EC4P 4EE
Copyright © Tim Kennemore 1983
Printed in Great Britain
by Richard Clay (The Chaucer Press) Ltd
Bungay, Suffolk

ISBN 0 416 50250 4

Contents

BOX OF TRICKS

Mrs. Whitney never knew what had caused her to order the book *The Pollution of Youth*. Pure chance, or subconscious instinct? It was certainly a most unlikely thing for her to possess. Somewhat nervously, she withdrew it from its cardboard wrapping. It was very big. The cover was a glossy white. Mrs. Whitney hardly dared touch it. For some years now she'd hardly read anything unless it was the book of something she'd seen on television, or a film star's biography – and not then if the print was too small. There was something very alarming about *The Pollution of Youth*. Squat and fat and chunky, it seemed to glow like some unearthly oracle.

Gingerly she flipped the cover back and scanned the contents page. The chapter headings were most unusual. "A Generation of Morons." "The Box in the Corner – Saccharin-Coated Sex and Violence." Mrs. Whitney blinked. "The Quarter-Pounder Mentality." What *was* this? And then she looked down to the last section, and saw: "How to Save Your Children." Her jaw dropped. She began to riffle through the pages. For, though she was not yet sure what they were to be saved from, she had long suspected that her children needed to be saved from something. And here was the proof. Perhaps she could save Joshua. He was only ten, after all; he might yet be retrievable. Mrs. Whitney wasn't so foolish as to imagine that she could possibly save Torby.

Torby, strangely enough, had been the cause of the whole thing. It had begun on a morning just such as this, a month ago, 4th July, Mrs. Whitney's birthday. Mrs. Whitney liked birthdays; she guarded hers jealously, and wrote "My Birthday" on her kitchen Make-a-Date calendar three weeks in advance. There was little chance that anyone would remember it otherwise. She went downstairs to find that Torby and Joshua had given her a birthday treat; they had put their TV Breakfasts in the oven themselves, rather than leave it for her to do. She was touched. So thoughtful. For a wild, optimistic moment she even imagined that they might leave the TV off, and sit at the table – she had a sudden vision of the family gathered around her, watching with glowing faces as she unwrapped her presents – but then she heard the familiar theme music "Start the Day the Happy Way" blare out from the sitting room, and knew the dream was in vain.

She pulled the disposable aluminium foil trays from the oven and took them through. "Breakfast!" she said, averting her eyes from the little pile of parcels on her table. It was so silly to be excited. She could predict their contents with deadly accuracy. Her husband would have given her a charm for her silver charm bracelet and a bottle of perfume (Moonlight Rapture); from Joshua there would be a box of chocolates (Black Magic) and from Torby a set of toiletries (lavender). And yet . . . her heart fluttered pleasurably.

Torby and Joshua, who were sitting on the floor eighteen inches away from the screen, held out their hands hungrily without shifting their gaze. Dexterously their mother slotted the trays between the impatient fingers – the one with the Original Oatmeal porridge for Torby, Chocolate porridge for Josh. Mrs. Whitney didn't like TV Breakfasts at all. She was convinced that anything which came out of aluminium foil was certain to damage the intestines, sooner or later. In her view you couldn't argue with bacon. But Torby's will, as ever, prevailed. Mrs. Whitney went back to the kitchen to make the coffee, and met her husband in the hall. He was looking apologetic. This did not bode well.

"Happy birthday, dear." He kissed her. She beamed.

"I'll just go and make us some coffee, and then I'll open my presents."

"Er ... um." He shifted uneasily from foot to foot. "Actually ... I'm so very sorry ... but I have to dash. The meeting, you know. I must see Mrs. Halsey first. Really, terribly important ..." he faltered. Mr. Whitney had recently been made a Departmental Head. For years this had been his greatest dream, the summit of his ambitions. Life, he felt, had no more to offer. "I'll see the presents tonight," he said encouragingly. Battling with waves of disappointment, Mrs. Whitney trailed after him to administer the regulation Peck on the Cheek with which Mr. Whitney was launched into the world on each working day.

"Your father had to go," she said to the back of Torby's neck, as she returned to the sitting room. Torby had already finished her Original Oatmeal and was deep into her Breakfast Crunch (genuine Toast and Marmalade flavour). She shrugged. It was all the same to her. In Torby's opinion her father had become far too chirpy since becoming a Departmental Head. He was starting to answer back. This would have to be checked. He had purchased a smart black Desk Set, comprising diary, table lighter, pen holder, calculator and a particularly pointless executive toy. He had taken to reading books with titles such as *Techniques in Delegation of Duty* and *Data Processing Part One*. Power wreaks havoc in the unlikeliest personality, thought Torby.

11

"Well. Shall I open my presents, then?" Grunts from the children. Mrs. Whitney hesitated; it was the One Thousand Plus Game Show. She couldn't hope to compete with that. She decided to open her cards first; the postman had brought the usual six or seven.

Five minutes later Louise Manning of Gidea Park had narrowly failed to win a brand new car. Subdued noises of approval from Torby and Joshua, who always wanted people to lose. They were by now slurping their Muesli Milk. "I'll open my presents, now," said Mrs. Whitney, hopefully, and, reaching for the first parcel, noticed for the first time that something was wrong, Three parcels only. There should be four. There were always four. Three parcels, and a brown envelope, on which was written in Torby's eccentric scrawl: "Happy Birthday, Mum." Mrs. Whitney didn't know what to do. Where were the toiletries (lavender)? What was happening? She decided to open the parcels first, as if the delay might cause the brown envelope to be magically transformed.

"Oh, Joshua, dear, chocolates! How sweet of you! And Black Magic, too. My *very* favourite."

"Grraanghh." said Joshua, without looking round. The Commuter of the Week Contest was on.

"Now, I wonder what your father's bought me ... oh, it's perfume! Moonlight Rapture ... and look, a little windmill for my charm bracelet." The sails spun round when she pushed them. It was very sweet. "Look, Torby."

"Uuuurgh," said Torby vaguely.

Mrs. Whitney was left with the envelope. What sort of present could you put in an envelope? She scratched her head, perplexed. Mrs. Whitney always had great difficulty coping with the unexpected. She resolved that, whatever it might be, she wouldn't be disappointed. One must never hurt the feelings of the giver. That was the thing.

Oh, do get on with it, thought Torby, leaning back and

propping herself up on her elbows. The Commuter of the Week was announced, and the programme switched to a live outside broadcast from the 7.24 from Southend to Liverpool Street, second carriage from the back. Mr. Harold Briggs, the lucky winner, was informed of his good fortune; up stepped last week's winner, Miss Penelope Finch from Orpington, to put the sash round his neck. Mr. Briggs looked very foolish in the sash. Mild applause from the other occupants of the carriage as the train rattled through Romford. Boring, thought Torby, and scowled. She hated commuters. They were like Space Invaders, sitting there in their little rows, all exactly alike, and when they got up their little legs went left, right, left, right, in perfect unison, relentlessly they marched on. You could fire lasers at them and still they'd keep on coming, all exactly alike, left, right...

"Oh Torby," said Mrs. Whitney. At last. "Torby, I don't understand."

Torby sighed, and went over to the table. "It's a Book Club. I've bought you a year's membership. The booklet shows you your opening choice, you can order any three of these. Then you get a new selection every month."

"Oh – Torby – that's very generous – but I don't ..."

"You're always saying," said Torby impassively, "how you mean to start reading again. How books are a treasure trove of untold riches."

Mrs. Whitney gulped sheepishly. It was true; she did say those things. But they weren't the sort of thing one expected anybody to take the slightest notice of. Still – how thoughtful of Torby. How kind. She felt a sentimental sob coming on; Torby moved discreetly out of hugging range.

Mrs. Whitney almost said: "But can you *afford* all this?" but remembered just in time that Torby could afford it very well. Torby was, in fact, rich. The reasons for this were twofold. At the age of seven Torby had decided to enter the

Junior Miss Pizza of London contest. As a result of her victory in this she went on to make a series of commercials for Parker's Piquant Pizzas. The commercials were very well paid. This happy state of affairs lasted for three years, until pizza suddenly went out of fashion, and Torby with it.

Then, a year ago, Great Aunt Beatrice Torby died, and left all her money to Torby. This came as a severe shock to Mr. Whitney; she was *his* great aunt, and he had rather expected to get the money himself. He and his wife puzzled over it for some time, eventually reaching the conclusion that Great Aunt Beatrice had based her decision on the fact that Torby had been named after her. Torby found this highly amusing. Only once had Great Aunt Beatrice mentioned the subject of names to her. "I bet you're glad they didn't call you Beatrice," she had said, chuckling. Torby had agreed to this, with feeling. Torby and the old lady understood each other perfectly. The real reason for the will, as Torby well knew, was that she was the only member of the family whom Great Aunt Beatrice considered worthy to inherit sixpence. Torby agreed with this, too.

Mrs. Whitney fingered her booklet and her order form.

"Look at the book selection," said Torby. Mrs. Whitney obeyed.

"Oooh! Oh, Torby, look! Judy Garland! The new book about Judy Garland!" Judy was Mrs. Whitney's great favourite. *The Wizard of Oz* reduced her to a soggy quivering blancmange, every time, and she'd seen it seventeen times, now.

"Yeah, I know."

"What do I do to order this?"

"Just put an X in the little box, there." Torby wondered how her mother had managed to reach her present great age all on her own, so helpless did she sometimes seem. "I'll

14

post it for you on the way to school. Which others do you want?"

"I don't know ... oh yes, look, *The Golden Years of Hollywood*. Oh, how nice!" she said, happily. She was starting to enjoy herself. She was discovering that she liked putting little X's in little boxes. "Now, one more." She looked and looked at the other titles, but nothing caught her eye. But Torby was hovering impatiently, so she quickly put a third X. The title by the box she had marked was *The Pollution of Youth*, by Francine Kazarian.

And now, a month later, here it was, shiny jacket shimmering in the slanting rays of the morning sun. Mrs. Whitney felt both repelled by and drawn to it. She had never possessed anything remotely like it before. *Judy Garland* and *The Golden Years of Hollywood* lay untouched. It was very strange. She must read this book.

Torby and Joshua were, as usual, flopped before the TV screen. The school holidays had begun, so it was later, nearly half past ten – not even Breakfast TV could induce them to leave their beds any earlier.

"I'm going round Jonathan's, Mum," said Joshua, lumbering to his feet.

"But you'll be back for lunch?"

"Nah, I'll have it at Jonathan's."

Mrs. Whitney sighed. She seemed to see even less of them in the holidays than during the term. "What about you, Torby? I was thinking of sausages."

"No, I'm meeting Sadie. We'll eat out."

Burgers, thought Mrs. Whitney. Burgers and cheesecake and Sweet and Savoury Ice Cream. That was all they wanted nowadays. She looked down at the book again, and gasped, for the chapter she had just turned to was called "The Rejection of Home Cooking". Startled, uneasy, she began to read.

15

Torby and Sadie went to the Funworld Amusement Centre in Hyde Park. They went into the Moonwalk and experienced one-sixth gravity; the Giant Twister turned them through 360 degrees five times in forty seconds.

"What now?" asked Sadie, sandy-haired bubbly Sadie, clutching what was left of her stomach. Most of it, she felt, was still in the Twister; she had a bit left, but it was almost certainly in the wrong place, and the wrong way up.

"Dunno. We've done almost everything. No – wait – what's that?"

"'The Human Body'," read Sadie. It seemed very apt. They staggered round the back of the Inter-Galaxia Dodgems. "The Latest Concept in Fun Rides," said the sign.

"Let's try it," said Torby. They would try anything, once.

"*Not* for the squeamish," said the grinning man who took their money. He was dressed as a surgeon. "Mats on the left." The mat was the exact colour and shape of a red blood corpuscle. They clambered through the bars of the ribcage and into the left lung; following the signs, they found their way into the pulmonary vein, sat on their corpuscles and whirled down into the left atrium of the heart.

"This way for the aorta," bellowed a guide. They dropped down through a valve into the ventricle, and were ushered into a car on a switchback, which conveyed its shrieking passengers around the cardio-vascular system to the remoter regions of the body, waltzing and looping around kidneys and spleen with a magnificent disregard for anatomical accuracy.

"What now?" asked Sadie again. Torby sighed. It was hard to know. Only a week into the holidays and already they seemed to have been everywhere, done everything. They'd *been* to the Silicon Centre, to Videoland, to the Wild West Theme Park (on Clapham Common), to Computer Games World, to Pinballopolis.

16

"It'd better be another Theme Bar, then." Sadie rummaged in her pocket and produced a piece of paper. "We've done all but six of them. Go on, you choose."

Torby scrutinized the list, weighing the pros and cons of the six as yet unvisited Theme Bars. They had sworn to visit every Theme Bar in London by September, and they were well on course. The Cricketer? Too far. The Will Shakespeare? No, Torby wanted to save that for last. "How about the Joan of Arc? It's in Foodland. We've not been to Foodland for ages. Ten days at least."

"Yeah, OK." Sadie thought of her suffering stomach, but Sadie's stomach had miraculous powers of recuperation, especially when she was in Foodland. "Good. We'll do that then. Foodland."

Foodland had taken London by storm. It had caused sociologists to speculate on the coming of the Gastronomic Revolution, and the implications of this for mankind. A street in the West End had been closed to traffic and converted into a pedestrian precinct; escalators spiralled, corkscrewlike, up to the second and third storeys. Londoners and tourists alike flocked in, seven days a week, through the magnificent archway with its famous signs: "Everything you Never Dreamed of" and "Liberate Your Taste Buds".

Torby and Sadie wandered in, and past the inevitable Sweet and Savoury Ice Cream Bar. These had erupted over the surface of the capital like a rash. A lighted sign in the window flashed out its message: "Welcome to the Gastronomic Mecca. Sweet to the Left, Savoury to the Right." They had recently introduced fluoride into the Sweet side. This, they claimed, more than offset the tooth-rotting properties of the sugar. Torby and Sadie headed for the Savoury side. Here, Flavour of the Day was Baked Bean. Torby had a theory that all this meant was they had a lot of surplus Baked Bean to get rid of. She bought a Double

Delight twin cone, one scoop cheese, one scoop pickled onion, the cone itself Tasty Spicy Fry. Sadie had curry flavour, extra-hot.

"If we eat quickly and walk slowly," she said, "we'll have finished by the time we get to the Cheesecake Centre." Torby nodded, and they ambled contentedly towards the escalator to the first floor – Foodlevel Two, it was called. Here was the 365 Cheesecake Centre. Cheesecake was enjoying a startling boom, coinciding with the decline in pizza. The Cheesecake Centre boasted that they had finally bridged the edibility gap; there were *no* foods that could not be eaten, in any combination, in the form of cheesecake.

"No, it's no good," said Sadie sadly. "I can't manage cheesecake and still have room for a burger."

"I can," said Torby, whose powers of consumption were phenomenal. She went and lolled against the counter, running her eyes up and down the list of 365 flavours in enjoyable anticipation. What should she have? Cinnamon Wine, Toad in the Hole, Onion Barbecue, Banana Custard, Sprouts and Gravy ... she decided to close her eyes and pick a number. It was the only way to choose.

Three hundred and thirteen. She looked. Squid. Oh. Well. Perhaps not. Perhaps they were out of squid. "I'll have a wedge of Sweet and Sour Chicken, and a wedge of Chocolate Mint," she said. Torby knew the terminology. Cheesecake on the spot was a slice; taken away it was a wedge. "D'you sell much squid?"

"I've never sold any," the boy said, scooping cheesecake into carton with a fish slice. "If you ask me it's just there to make up the 365 Flavours. Don't forget your tokens."

Torby went out, bearing her wedges – as she passed through the Exit door a recorded voice crooned: "Thank you for your custom; have a nice day and come again soon to the Cheesecake Centre" – and carefully folded her tokens away in her purse. Twenty-five tokens entitled you to a

18

sweatshirt in a choice of ten colours; accumulate fifty and you became a Super-Consumer, and 365 would deliver a giant cheesecake, in any flavour, to your home. Torby was currently awaiting delivery of her first giant cheesecake, and already had four tokens on the way to the next.

The final treat only awaited the digestion of the cheesecake. The Theme Burger Bars were the very latest craze. The Will Shakespeare had been the first of them; customers sat in a replica of the Globe Theatre to consume their Hamletburgers, or Macbeth's Head in a Basket, while Festes and Touchstones pranced in foolish motley. Once a day, at what time nobody ever knew, the Ghost of Hamlet's Father walked. The Will Shakespeare's success had been phenomenal; the Press reported that a minor Royal Personage dined there regularly, and all the plain Burger Bars in the country rushed to leap on the bandwagon. Soon there was the Jack the Ripper, where you were served by heavy-footed policemen, and the only form of cutlery provided was knives; the Gymnast, with its Double Piked Backburgers and Korbut's Fingers; the Solar System, where the tables revolved gracefully around a glowing sun, while speakers piped the music of Holst. Newest of all was the Guy Fawkes, tastefully situated directly under the Houses of Parliament. Senior members of both Houses had protested violently about this, but to no avail.

Torby and Sadie now found themselves outside the Joan of Arc Burnt-at-the Steak House – Fried French with your French Fried. Mrs. Whitney had been horrified when she heard about this. It was shocking, she said: blasphemous, corrupting and a sign of the times. It would not have been allowed when she was a girl. Mr. Whitney had commented, mildly, that it was harmless enough; he had seen far worse things in Soho. This remark startled Torby. She had once calculated that her father made, on average, one interesting remark a month; this was his contribution for May.

They were shown to their seats by the Bishop of Beauvais, Levi shoes poking out from beneath his robe. Fleurs-de-lys hung from the walls; in a corner a fire crackled, as yet Joanless. They studied the menu. Joan Rare. Joan Flambée, with Faggots. Hot Cross Joan. Joan Surprise. "What's Joan Surprise?" wondered Torby.

"Ask the Bishop," said Sadie, who was happily feeling a resurgence of appetite. Torby did so. The Bishop, who was hovering courteously, told her that if mademoiselle wished to know, mademoiselle would have to buy one. His accent was pure Kilburn. Mademoiselle, on reflection, ordered a Crispy Joanburger. "Make that two, bartender," said Sadie, trying out her American accent. The Bishop blinked, and retreated.

"How's your mother?" asked Sadie, and straight away burst into a fit of giggles. Mrs. Whitney was a source of endless hilarity. Sometimes Torby only had to say, in a particular, lugubrious tone: "My mother says ..." and Sadie would be off into hysterics.

"Her Book Club choice came today," said Torby. The Crispy Joanburgers arrived; predictably, they were just any old burger, except for the fleur-de-lys picked out on top in sesame seeds, and the stake driven through the middle. "Remember – my birthday present. It nearly finished her, not getting toiletries, lavender. I thought she was going to collapse." Sadie spluttered. "When I left she was reading some weird thing about pollution. Doubt if she'll get beyond the first page."

"Pollution?" Sadie mused. "You don't mean *The Pollution of Youth*?"

"Yeah, that was it. Why? How come you've heard of it?"

"Oh, Torby, you must know about *The Pollution of Youth*. It was written by this weird American professor woman who's taken all her five children to live in a sort of hut in the middle of nowhere. She thinks that modern society is destroying our morals. There was a thing about her on telly the other night. The book's terribly famous."

"Oh, *that* book. Yeah, I saw it. They filmed the kids, chopping firewood. They were supposed to be enjoying it."

"Weird," said Sadie. "Weird" was a favourite word of theirs. "And they've got no television – nothing. Miles from a Macdonalds even. God, they must be so *bored*."

"Weird," said Torby. "Crackpot Professors. Almost as bad as commuters. So that's what she's reading, is it? I bet it's full of big big words. She'll never finish the first chapter."

"Super-weird," said Sadie, and choked.

Mrs. Whitney sat and read the first six chapters of *The Pollution of Youth* straight through. This feat took her three hours, and she almost forgot about making the pie for dinner. It was most disturbing, this book. All the mistakes she had made! And look at the results! "A Generation of Morons!" thundered Professor Kazarian. Well, Torby certainly wasn't a moron. Torby had wonderful brains, which her mother supposed she had inherited from Great Aunt Beatrice, who had been such a demon on the stock market. No, Torby wasn't a moron. But ... Joshua, she thought uneasily, weighing the flour for the pastry. "Did you tell your children bedtime stories?" demanded Professor Kazarian. "Did you sing them lullabies?" Mrs. Whitney had a vivid memory of attempting to sing a lullaby to Torby; Torby, aged not quite three, had said: "Go 'way, Mummy, I'm trying to sleep." Was it her fault if...

The doorbell rang. Mrs. Whitney went to answer it, wiping her hands. It was a man; a man with a colourful wedge-shaped hat that said, "365 Flavours."

"Mocha Pistachio," he said cheerfully to Mrs. Whitney. "Shall I bring it in for you?" The cheesecake was deposited on the kitchen table. Mrs. Whitney looked at it. "Happy consuming," said the delivery man. "I'll see myself out."

Mrs. Whitney sidled up to the cheesecake. It was so very big. It was nearly as wide as the table. She edged around it, turned her back and tried to get on with her pastry, but the cheesecake had a definite Presence, and she was unable to stop herself giving it sidelong glances, to see that it had not moved closer. She couldn't concentrate on the pastry. The pie would be ruined.

She turned and looked the cheesecake squarely in the eye. Now, what to do? What would her husband do? He wouldn't notice it. What would Torby do? She would eat it. "What would you do?" she asked her rubber plant. And, instantly, she knew.

Mrs. Whitney had a secret. When she was on her own she talked to her rubber plant, which she called Liza. She had heard that they liked it. And lately she had been on her own so much that she often found herself chattering to Liza for hours on end; Liza was thriving, with all this attention. Perhaps the cheesecake could be won round in the same way.

She approached the table, cleared her throat and said: "Hello! My, you're a pretty thing!" in a rather hesitant voice. But there – now the ice was broken. "Did you have far to come? I'm sorry Torby wasn't here to welcome you . . ." She drew the pastry board and rolling pin over and began to shape the pie crust. "She's out, being polluted." Mrs. Whitney was learning fast. She smiled at the cheesecake. It was quite a nice thing, really. "I'm sure you'll like Torby. She's very unusual, if I do say it myself."

By the time Torby came in, Mrs. Whitney and the cheesecake were great friends.

"Doesn't it look smashing?" Torby twirled it round with admiration.

"Oh, it *is*," Mrs. Whitney said, and then gasped in horror as Torby went for it with a knife. "Don't!"

"Don't what?" mumbled Torby through a Mocha Pistachio mouthful. Mrs. Whitney turned away. Torby shrugged; her mother was becoming quite peculiar, she sometimes thought.

Joshua came in then, and the two of them settled down, instantly, in front of the television. "Your father expects to be back for tea at six, tonight," said their mother. This was not a sufficiently rare occurrence to deserve comment. "Grrumph," said Torby.

Mrs. Whitney thought of the book, and how it condemned television, and recommended Family Games as a far more valuable pastime. She pondered. A game of Monopoly would be nice – she hadn't played Monopoly for years. But the thought of trying to explain Monopoly to Joshua brought her up short. One mustn't be over-ambitious. Perhaps Scrabble. She opened her mouth to suggest it, but at that moment the theme music of *Hypermarket* began, and her mouth closed again. *Hypermarket* was *Hypermarket*. She would try later. Meanwhile, she'd read some more of the book.

Hypermarket was a potent drug. Addicts who had tried to give it up had reported severe withdrawal symptoms: rashes, cold sweats, anxiety attacks. It was a day-by-day saga of ordinary people in a big store. Would Deputy Manageress Lily discover that Unloading-Boy Peter was the baby she had given up for adoption twenty years before? Was the Delicatessen aisle really haunted by the ghost of former Manager Genevieve, who had been mortally impaled on a shard of glass when the Hypermarket window was smashed? Was it Store Detective Jason's delinquent son who had smashed it? And was Jason an undercover agent, planted by a rival store? Why were so many packets of frozen filleted fish disappearing without a trace? And who, oh who, was putting the poison pen letters in the ten pound note compartment of Checkout Polly's till? As fast as one mystery was unravelled, further complications set in.

Mrs. Whitney, half watching, half reading, felt a sudden surge of indignation against the television. Nasty little box! It had enslaved her children! Mrs. Whitney was at least a *selective* viewer. She watched a great many old films – the Hollywood musicals she loved so much. But she *chose* to watch them. Torby and Joshua just watched anything that came on. Why, if she were to speak to them, this very moment, neither of them would hear her. She would test it. "Knickers!" she said loudly. Nothing. They were deaf to all but *Hypermarket*. Sadly, almost desperately, she recalled the Professor's terrible words about images from the media ... decline in standards ... self-indulgent pleasure-seeking society ... brainwashing ... How simple, how desirable, a family game of Scrabble suddenly seemed. The Professor would approve. After dinner, she resolved.

Hypermarket ended; in walked Mr. Whitney, clutching *Data Processing Part One*. This was proving heavy going; it was beginning to seem unlikely that he would ever make it to *Part Two*. "That book," muttered Mrs. Whitney, and served the pie.

The pie did at least have the effect of uniting the family around the table for a while, although Torby and Joshua were shovelling it away with the greatest possible speed, and Mr. Whitney had *Data Processing Part One* balanced against his sideplate and was reading while he ate. Judging by his expression, the combination of pie and Data Processing was particularly indigestible.

"Have a nice day at work, dear?"

"... retrieved from the data bank. Pardon?"

"Never mind. Oh – Torby. Aren't you going to finish your pie?"

"Had enough," said Torby. "We had Crispy Joanburgers, out. Very filling."

"Joanburgers..." Mrs. Whitney pursed her lips.

24

"And the cheesecake," said Joshua, who had done rather well out of the cheesecake himself.

"*Don't mention the cheesecake!*" said Mrs. Whitney, painfully. And Joanburgers. It was indecent. It was just exactly what the Professor was saying. Her face, as she did the washing up, was deeply thoughtful. Mr. Whitney had long since disappeared, with a huge pile of books and papers. They wouldn't see him again all evening.

When she returned to the sitting room Torby and Joshua were busy playing one of Torby's seemingly endless collection of television games. Mrs. Whitney considered these a supreme waste of money. The two of them would spend hours sprawled in front of the set, playing Space Invaders, Tele-Pinball, Football, Dodgems, Roulette, Astro Wars, Drag Racing – they broke the bank at Monte Carlo, quelled mutinies on Jupiter and crashlanded on asteroids, without ever moving from their own front room. And the games were all so garish, and so noisy. At present they were playing Battle of Zardon, one of the very noisiest. Torby, as usual, was winning; every time she destroyed one of Joshua's cruise missiles there was an ear-shattering bang, and the screen exploded in green, silver and purple.

"Torby," said Mrs. Whitney.

"There goes your command ship," said Torby. "What d'you say, Mum?"

Mrs. Whitney drew a breath. "I thought we might have a nice game of Scrabble."

"There goes the fuel," said Joshua dolefully. "What's Scrabble, Torby? You didn't tell me you'd got a new cartridge."

"I haven't," said Torby, zapping a missile. Explosion.

"It's a board game," said Mrs. Whitney. "You play it on a board, Josh."

"Huh? How does it plug into the telly?"

"It doesn't."

Joshua frowned. This was a difficult concept for him to grasp. "Battery," he said at last. "Oh, flippin' heck, Torby." He watched the screen glumly; his entire space fleet lay in ruins, his planet was doomed.

"No batteries," said Mrs. Whitney.

"How's it work, then?"

"You work it yourself. Look, Joshua. You have little tiles with letters on, and you put them on the board to make words ... you spell out words, you see..." Her voice faded, as she met Joshua's eyes.

"That's supposed to be *fun*?" He spoke with a mixture of bewilderment and scorn. Spelling was a great mystery to Joshua: a mystery which could, for all he cared, remain for ever unsolved.

Mrs. Whitney reconsidered. Perhaps Joshua wasn't quite up to Scrabble. "We might play Snap," she said. This earned her a withering glare from Torby. Oh, dear. What could you *do*, when the members of your family were all at such different *levels*? These families who played games together – what on earth did they play? She felt she had let the Professor down.

"You see," she said, "in this book, Josh, it says that..." This was a serious mistake. Joshua leaped back as if she had offered him a scorpion. Joshua disliked and mistrusted books more than almost anything. They were the source of a great deal of botheration for him; he avoided them whenever possible.

"Snakes and ladders," Mrs. Whitney said, feebly.

"It's the Incredible Dissolving Woman now," said Joshua with an air of great finality, and switched to BBC 1. The subject was closed. Mrs. Whitney felt helpless and useless and pointless. She went to bed early, and *The Pollution of Youth* went with her.

She read and read till she fell asleep. She read all through the chapters about television; the Box in the Corner. This made a deep impression on her; it seemed, suddenly, as if television was to blame for every single thing that was wrong with her family. Greed and discontent, she thought. Images from the media; saccharin-coated sex and violence. Torby's eccentricity, her husband's remoteness, Joshua's – well, Joshua's everything, could be traced to this single cause. The cathode-ray fiend. It was the twentieth century equivalent of bubonic plague. Her poor children. They had never stood a chance.

"She was *really* weird this morning," said Torby, slicing into her Gunpowder Grill. "Gazing at the wall; glazed eyes."

"Oh *dear*," said Sadie, with delight. "Very bad signs."

"Very bad. And last night! When I came in I'll swear she was talking to my cheesecake. Oh, and Sade, you should have seen her – bobbing up and down like a rubber duck trying to get us to play Scrabble!"

"She must have been reading *The Pollution of Youth* after all," said Sadie, and turned her attention to her Plotburger. It was really good here at the Guy Fawkes. They were seated at a large barrel; every so often a rocket would go off with a great swoosh of coloured sparks. Skulking in corners were men; dark, muffled men. Five minutes before, some other men had rushed in, and with cries of "Got you!" they had hustled the skulking men away. But already they were beginning to creep back, to whisper – to skulk. It was very atmospheric, thought Sadie.

"It must be a very stupid book," said Torby.

"It is," said Sadie. "Oh, look, they're coming to light the bonfire." Another rocket went off, deafeningly. "There goes Guy!"

"Weird," said Torby, with relish.

The front door banged; Torby went straight through to the kitchen.

"Oh, it's you, Torby."

"So it is." Torby never ceased to wonder at her mother's powers of observation.

"Cheese salad for dinner," said her mother, "and I've made a ginger pudding."

"Oh, good," said Torby absently. "Actually, I'm not all that hungry. We called in at the Gymnast on the way home, and had some Korbut's Fingers."

"Korbut's..." No. She wouldn't ask. It was better not to know.

"Delicious," said Torby. "Mum, why are you trembling?"

"Trembling?" said Mrs. Whitney, trembling. "I'm not trembling."

"You look like a jelly with Parkinson's disease," said Torby, and went through to put the televison on for *Hypermarket*. The television wasn't there. "Mum? Did the telly conk out? *Mum?*"

Mrs. Whitney appeared in the doorway. "No," she said. "No, it didn't. I've – I've got rid of it, Torby."

"You've *what?*" Torby gaped. This was ridiculous. She wanted to watch *Hypermarket*. Well, she'd just go and watch it on her own set. She wasn't going to stand here arguing with a demented parent. She marched upstairs to her bedroom.

Her set wasn't there, either.

"Mum!" This was *outrageous*.

"It's no good, Torby." Mrs. Whitney tried to sound firm. "I've got rid of that too." She hadn't actually got *rid* of them. Mrs. Whitney simply hadn't been able to work out just how one got rid of two perfectly good television sets within the space of a few hours, so she'd carried them out to the garden shed and covered them with a tarpaulin. "It was destroying our family life, Torby!"

"Mum, that was *my television*. Mine. I *paid* for it." Torby just couldn't believe this. It was laughable, illogical as a dream.

"You will be reimbursed." said her mother. "Every penny. But as long as I'm under this roof there will be no televisions here!" She quavered, with a sudden vision of Torby throwing her out.

"OK," said Torby. "Fine." She came downstairs and went to the front door.

"Where are you going?"

"To Sadie's," said Torby.

"But the salad; the ginger pudding..."

"I said I wasn't hungry." The door slammed. Mrs. Whitney shuddered. But it could have been worse. She hadn't been physically attacked; the rest of the house was still intact. There was still Joshua to face, but if she could cope with Torby she could certainly cope with Joshua. She was determined not to relent. She had made up her mind. They'd thank her for it, one day.

Sadie's mother drove Torby home after the late night movie. Sadie's mum liked Torby. And no sooner had Torby clambered into bed than there was a timid knocking on the door and in slunk Joshua, a miserable, desperate, anguished Joshua. "Oh, Torby," he said straight away, "what're you gonna do, Torby?" He didn't say "we". Whatever was to be done, Torby would do it.

"Sit down," said Torby, "and don't panic."

"Oh, it was awful, Torby! I wanted to go round Jonathan's but she wouldn't let me – and, Torby, I missed *Hypermarket*! And she kept on at me to play Continuo so I threw the cards at her and then she let me alone."

"What did Dad say?"

"He didn't even notice it had gone! Torby, what're you gonna do? She's got rid of them, Torby!"

"No she hasn't," said Torby. "Mrs. Beasley was out in

29

the garden and saw her putting them in the shed. It's all over the street by now."

Joshua brightened. "Then we can go and get them back!"

"No we can't. She'll only take them out there again."

Joshua considered. "Then we hit her."

"Violence never solved anything," said Torby, primly. "No. What I'm going to do is to fix it so that *she* goes and fetches them back."

"How you gonna do that, Torby?"

"I've done it," said Torby. "I phoned from Sadie's, and I just caught them. You wait till tomorrow, and you'll see. By midday those televisions will be back."

"Midday? What about the breakfast show? What'll we do for breakfast, Torby?"

"You'll manage," said Torby. "Bear up."

The postman brought another brown envelope in the morning. Mrs. Whitney took it into the sitting room. She was expecting a row, but all was silence. Torby and Joshua were sitting on the floor in the usual positions, gazing at the wall. It was most unnerving. But better than a row. Perhaps they were coming round. She opened the envelope.

"Torby? What's this? The Video Club? I don't belong to the Video Club."

"Yes you do. If you join the Book Club you automatically become a member of the Video Club," lied Torby. Thank God they'd caught the post.

"You mean ... I ..." Mrs. Whitney gazed at the booklet in stunned disbelief. It was offering her films. Movies. The things she loved best in the world. "Oh, Torby, how wonderful! Is it just like the Book Club? Order three – put little X's in little boxes?"

"Yeah, that's right."

"*The Sound of Music!*" She was in raptures. "Oh, that's so

30

lovely – you know *The Sound of Music*, Torby?"

"Yeah, singing nuns."

Mrs. Whitney marked in a little X. "Now, let's see – oh, yes, *Love Story*. I always have a lovely cry when I see that." Torby knew it. She winced. Weeping and wailing, and Julie Andrews running over mountains and hugging trees. A heavy price to pay. But it would be worth it.

"*The Wizard of Oz*," said Mrs. Whitney, faintly. It was too much. "Torby. My very own *Wizard of Oz* ... I can see it whenever I want ... any time of the day or night ..."

"Yes, indeed," said Torby, trying not to mind. She didn't think she could stomach a Munchkin, before breakfast.

"I wonder what they do about a machine," said Mrs. Whitney, this aspect of the matter striking her at long last. "Do they send me a projector, Torby? It doesn't say."

"Oh, Mum, really. You weren't expecting a reel of film, were you? They're cartridges. You just slot them into the video recorder."

"Oh yes, of course. I ..." And then she realized that the video recorder was attached to the television.

"That's that, then," said Torby. "May as well tear it up. What a waste of a birthday present. Still."

Torby's present, thought Mrs. Whitney, in agonies. Dear, thoughtful Torby. Never hurt the feelings of the giver, she thought. All her life she had tried to live by that principle. She glanced down at the booklet; Judy Garland seemed to dance before her eyes. Movies – such innocent, harmless pleasure ... had she perhaps been a little hasty? Television could, after all, be so educational. You could learn a lot. And the documentaries ... she would see to it that in future they watched more documentaries. She looked up at Torby, who was softly humming 'Over the Rainbow'. Torby shrugged.

When she'd fetched the televisions in, Mrs. Whitney took *The Pollution of Youth* and stuffed it firmly into the very back of her least-used cupboard. The book was a trouble-maker and a stirrer. Best forgotten. And then she sat down and put her third and final little X in a little box.

DIMINISHED THIRDS

If, at the beginning of this term, someone had asked me to bet on what would be the most awful lesson in it, I would confidently have staked my last penny on its being a Biology lesson with Mrs. Macrae. Any of us would. It would never even have entered my head that it might turn out to be a Music lesson, Music with skinny little Miss Pindock, tucked away in her room on the top floor with her metronomes, her xylophones and her sheet music copies of "Cherry Ripe". Just as well, then, that there never was any bet, or I should now be totally bankrupt.

The only word to describe Miss Pindock's lessons is boring. The moment I stepped into that room of hers I could feel my eyes glazing over in anticipation of the boredom to come. There she would be, sitting at her piano, with her flat chest and her flat face, her little round glasses welded to her head – she had certainly been born with them, and with the tight, flat little bun that perched on the back of her head. She had been born aged fifty-five; she was unchanging and unchangeable. We suspected that she lived up here in the Music Room, leaving it only to scuttle down in the morning to play the hymn at Assembly. At night, she slept in the cupboard, clutching a boxed set of Beethoven's symphonies to her maidenly bosom. This was Miss Pindock.

The nature, though not the degree, of the boredom had varied slightly over the years. In the first year we did a lot of Creative Music-Making. Miss Pindock would dole out the instruments strictly according to musical ability – the lowest grade being the triangle – Margaret Dyson would lead the singing, and away we went, bang, crash, ting-a-ling. I always had a triangle. My friend Tin, who's the daughter of the Sum Ling Chinese Takeaway in North Street, was favoured by Miss Pindock, and permitted to play the glockenspiel. She would sit there doing her inscrutable Oriental bit, which I think Miss Pindock found impressive. There was once talk of our doing 'Lord of the Dance' at Assembly, but nothing ever came of it. And so passed the first boring year.

In the second year we put away these childish things and progressed to Musical Appreciation. This meant that Miss Pindock played records, uplifting, educational classical records to us, while we sat in rows, and appreciated. The one good thing about this was that Miss Pindock would go off into a sort of trance, so we could make sensible use of the time by reading our homework chapter for history, or stimulating the intellect with a game of hangman, while Lisa Hennessey and Co. drooled their way through their True Life Romance magazines.

The exception to all this was Margaret Dyson, who went off into a trance along with Miss Pindock; but you have to make allowances for Margaret, she's a sort of musical genius, a budding soprano, not to mention being the only Third Year ever to be first violin in the school orchestra. I once overheard her having a conversation with Miss Pindock about things called diminished thirds and minor triads; she's also rumoured to be writing a rock opera in her spare time. I must say in her defence that in all other respects she's quite normal.

And so, the minutes would limp past. A few hundred eternities later the record player would snap off; simultaneously, Miss Pindock snapped out of her trance, and we snapped our attention smartly from the Agricultural Revolution and prepared to tell Miss Pindock all about how much we had appreciated this masterly, divine work of Mozart (or Tchaikovsky, or Schubert – we would jot the composer down at the start of the lesson, so that we would, at the end, know whom we had been appreciating). That was marvellous, Miss Pindock; absolutely sublime, Miss Pindock. And Miss Pindock would be pleased.

The seeds of the fateful lesson were sown in the one before it. The end of term was fast approaching, and Miss Pindock had decided that we should practise the school song in readiness for its annual, final-Assembly-of-the-year rendering. "Gather round the piano, girls."

Reluctantly we gathered. I particularly hate singing. My voice is tuned differently from other people's. Me singing a scale is like a car climbing a steep hill; at two strategic points I have to change gear, and I must have really bad clutch control because the resulting noise is fearful, fearful. So I keep a wise silence, and merely move my lips. Today, it seemed that half the class had the same idea. Those who were singing, were singing particularly badly, even by our far from spectacular standards. The school song was being murdered; it was slowly being tortured to death, a fate, incidentally, it has long deserved.

Miss Pindock didn't think so. "'Thand'?" she cried in dismay. "'Pand'? What, 3K, are 'Thand' and 'Pand'?" Nobody was prepared to tell her. "With *strength*," she said, "and *hope*, and *spirit*" – clipping the ends of 'strength' and 'hope' ruthlessly away. This line always gets us. Miss Pindock has an obsession about it. "I want to *hear*," she said hopefully, "where one word ends and the next begins. You are *slurring*, 3K. Slovenly singing! Again!"

"With streng," we sang, "thand hoe, pand spirit..."

"No, no!" Miss Pindock buried her head in her hands. This was always a very bad sign. "3K, what is the matter with you? You aren't the girls you were last year. I used to look forward to my lessons with 2K, always so bright, so lively. But since you became 3K – where has all the effort gone? The enthusiasm? The *life*?" She flashed a look at Margaret Dyson to say, it's all right dear, you're excluded from all this, I don't mean you, but really, dear, I'm nearing the end of my tether!

She was right, of course, we *were* different, and there was a reason for it, but not a reason that could possibly be explained to her. It was simple. Last year, we had had Music second lesson on Tuesdays, just after English with Miss Miles. This year, Music comes last thing on a Wednesday, directly after double Biology with Mrs. Macrae. To anyone who knew these two ladies the whole thing would be instantly clear. Eighty minutes of uninterrupted, unalleviated Mrs. Macrae was like going fifteen rounds with Mohammad Ali. By the time we had all staggered, punch-drunk and reeling, up to the Music Room, we were in no fit state for anything. We needed to be treated very, very gently.

Miss Pindock had no notion of this. "I've had *enough*," she said, shutting the piano. "You're wasting my time. I'm very disappointed in you, 3K, very disappointed indeed. I think we'll just listen to some music until the bell goes."

Resigned, chastened, we dragged our chairs back to the desks, while Miss Pindock, her back quivering slightly with wounded indignation, went to select the recording which was to brighten the final twenty minutes of our school day. "Dvorak," she said. "Symphony No. 5, in E minor, opus 95. 'From the New World.'" The record player clicked on and away went Dvorak; Miss Pindock settled herself in her chair in the pre-trance position; the class went into their Appreciation routine. All was as usual. Or so it seemed.

"Alison Lowe!"

"Hup – yerp – yes, Miss Pindock?" The Lisa Hennessey camp shot bolt upright in alarm.

"*What* is *that*?"

"Yerp," bleated Alison Lowe. Tin and I exchanged interested glances; I could see Tin filing the fact away: Alison Lowe, when startled, goes 'yerp'. Miss Pindock rose majestically to her full five foot four, strode to the record player and silenced Dvorak. It was a very terrible silence. Then, only then, did she walk to Alison, hand outstretched before her. "Yerp, Miss Pindock," said Alison, and handed over her magazine.

"Well," said Miss Pindock. "Well. *True Love*," she read. "'Real life stories of heart-breaking and passionate romance.' Indeed, Alison. Indeed."

You had to feel some sympathy for Alison, vile little Lisa Hennessey toady-crawly-crony though she was. Never before had the trance failed to happen; you come to take these things for granted. Perhaps being near the end of her tether made Miss Pindock somehow trance-resistant. But we'd all made the same mistake; it could easily have been any of us.

Miss Pindock, now, seemed barely capable of speech. "Alison," she finally managed. "Why, Alison? Why?"

"Miss Pindock," said Lisa Hennessey. This was a disappointment; I had been looking forward to a succession of yerps. "Miss Pindock, it's just that it's always the same music."

"I beg your pardon, Lisa. I have never previously played the 'New World Symphony' to you. I . . ."

"No, Miss Pindock, it's just that it's always the same *kind* of music. I mean, we never listen to anything *modern*, do we?"

"Schoenberg?" said Miss Pindock.

"No, you know, Miss Pindock, pop. Pop music. That's music too, isn't it?" We were all nodding, making agreeing noises. Marie Newell, sitting next to Alison, joined in the attack.

"There was a programme on telly the other night, right, there was this school who'd got a steel band going. In music lessons, they did things like that. It was really good."

"We have no persons of Caribbean origin in this class," said Miss Pindock, faintly. She'd quite forgotten she was supposed to be giving Alison Lowe an almighty row. She was on the defensive, and running for cover.

"But it's nearly the end of *term*, Miss Pindock."

"Yes, Lisa," Miss Pindock said uncertainly, pondering the relevance of this remark.

"Couldn't we just once have pop music? I mean, as it's the end of term, and that. We could bring some records and you could appreciate them. It'd be really good."

"You mean, listen to pop music," Miss Pindock said, cleverly grasping the situation.

"Just *once*. Oh, please, Miss Pindock," Lisa said in an awful whiny little-girl voice. "Yeah," people were saying with enthusiasm, "go on, Miss Pindock." Miss Pindock looked round. You could see her thinking, the wheels going round clickety-click. Perhaps if I let them do this they'll change back to the nice girls they used to be. They might come alive again. Some spark may be rekindled.

"Yes," she said. "Very well, Lisa. I shall be most interested to hear your records. I'm sure it'll be very enjoyable. Very enjoyable." She really looked as if she meant it. She's not such a bad old thing; only a few million centuries out of date.

Tin and I caught up with Lisa and Co. in the corridor.

"Sarah's got some good records," said Tin.

"I don't mind bringing some," I said. "I've got the Tim

38

Rice and Andrew Lloyd Webber ones, *Evita*, and *Jesus Christ Superstar*. I think she'd like those. And the Electric Light Orchestra – that's sort of, well – orchestral, in places – make her feel at home. Or a bit of Tubular Bells . . ."

"Oh, do shut up, Cunningham," said Lisa.

"Shut up yourself, Hennessey," said Tin.

"And you get lost and all, Egg Foo Yong. You two can keep out of this. It's nothing to do with you. We fixed it up, didn't we? *We*'ll choose the records."

"Yeah, s'right," muttered the other three, the chorus line. Tin was starting to look vicious.

"You're welcome," I said. "I don't want my records getting bust or scratched anyway." It was true. I wouldn't have trusted Lisa Hennessey within a mile of my records. I wouldn't have trusted her with a piece of used chewing gum.

"Old bitch kept my magazine," said Alison, making a V-sign over her shoulder.

Tin looked her squarely in the eye, and said, "Oh, yerp."

The week rolled by in a frivolous, end-of-the-year fashion. Collections for teachers who were leaving; Sports Day, which would have been dull but for a stray First Year who narrowly missed being impaled on a javelin, and was carried off in a dead faint. Everyone enjoyed that. Then Wednesday came, and, oh joy and jubilation, Mrs. Macrae wasn't there. Mrs. Macrae isn't one to stay home for a sniffle, so we were all hoping like mad that it was something serious, like death. So we were in buoyant mood when we arrived in the rarefied atmosphere of the Music Room. This was going to be smashing. Forty minutes of listening to music we actually liked. As far as I knew, we were the first form ever to find a chink in Miss Pindock's antediluvian armour.

She had the record player all ready. "You know, 3K," she said, rather shyly, "I'm really quite looking forward to this.

I'll be very interested to hear some of your music." Well, good for her; she had the right attitude. The old bat was making an effort. "May I have the records, then, Lisa. . . ?"

"Oh no, Miss Pindock," said Lisa, shocked, waving the box of records they had been guarding so carefully all day. "We'll do all the work, Miss Pindock. We want you just to sit back and enjoy it."

"But," said Miss Pindock, glancing at the record player in some alarm.

"Oh, don't worry," said Marie Newell, "Lisa's got one exactly the same as that at home, haven't you, Lisa? Come on, Miss Pindock, you deserve a rest. We'll do it."

"Well – yes, yes, very well. Very considerate." Nodding like a mandarin, Miss Pindock went over to her chair and sat obediently. Alison, Marie and Jennifer, meanwhile, had dragged their chairs out and planted themselves in a row at the front, alongside Lisa. That, apparently, was all they were going to do: just sit there, looking important – see, you out there, we're running this class. They always had to be noticed, Lisa's lot: always out front, the centre of attention. When we had form debates, it generally ended up being Lisa and Alison, for the motion, versus Marie and Jennifer, against the motion, or some other permutation thereof. If, by some mischance, another group was given the starring role, they would set to work to disrupt the lesson, thereby making themselves the centre of attention anyway. Tin says they're pathetic; they're just spoilt children. This is probably why they hate Tin so much; they can't impress her. Whatever they do, she sees right through them.

Lisa stood up, with ceremony. "The first record," she announced, "is 'Black Mass' by the Exorcists." Miss Pindock, who had been smiling benevolently, looked a little taken aback at this. Her expression became ever so slightly pained as she watched the sacred turntable, on which Bach, Johann Sebastian, and Handel, George Frederic,

40

were wont to revolve. Now supplanted by the Exorcists.

"Bit heavy to start with, I'd have thought," muttered Tin.

"Umph," I said, noncommittally, never having heard of the Exorcists, let alone this single.

I hope I never hear it again. It was terrible. It was one of the worst noises I've ever heard; it made a pneumatic drill sweet and harmonious by comparison. It was a screeching, senseless, discordant unholy row. The lyrics, which were shrieked rather than sung, and sounded more like the ravings of a demented hyena than anything human, were totally incomprehensible. Considering the subject matter, this was perhaps just as well.

I hardly dared look at Miss Pindock. But she hadn't flinched. You really had to hand it to her – she was trying so very hard to enjoy it. There was still the ghost of a determined smile on her face, and she was even making a half-hearted attempt to tap her foot to the rhythm. This of course was doomed to failure; there wasn't any rhythm. And then, it suddenly occurred to me that she hadn't the slightest idea that almost everyone in the room was hating the record just as much as she was. She thought we were really enjoying it; she was trying her hardest not to be a killjoy.

The next record was an improvement: an up-tempo disco number. From the speakers an insistent black voice implored Miss Pindock to shake her bootee, and to strut her funky stuff. Disappointingly she failed to comply, but the foot was tapping now with more conviction. I leaned back, flashed a quick smile at Tin, and began to relax.

Rule One for human survival: *Never relax.* Because straight away Lisa and her three grinning gaping ghouls went in for the kill. The series of records that followed could have been sent registered delivery from Hell. The Dead Dachshunds were succeeded by the Sebaceous Cysts, who gave way to the Vermin. And now Miss Pindock gave up; she could pretend no longer. She sat there, all hunched up, face pale and lips pressed tightly together. It sounds as if it might have been funny, but it wasn't – it was embarrassing. All round the room people were cringing, wriggling in discomfort. Tin was sitting immobile as a statue, her eyes fixed with loathing and scorn on the smirking Lisa Hennessey. The whole rotten four of them were smirking away up there. They thought they'd been really clever.

I buried my face in my hands, my index fingers jammed into my ears in a vain attempt to block out the relentless, cacophonous din. Each time a record ended my spirits rose slightly; I peeked out through my fingers, thinking, surely this time they'll put on a nice record, something with a tune, something bearable – and then would start a song called "Putrefied Matter" or "Rigor Mortis", and with a stifled groan I covered my ears again.

She had trusted us, that was the thing. She'd given us this chance to build a bridge between her music and ours – and who knows what that might have led to, next year? – and we'd blown it, blown the bridge sky-high. She'd been looking forward to it – she'd been all prepared to take an interest, she'd met us halfway. And we'd done this to her. No matter that most of the form hadn't known about it and were therefore technically innocent. We were all guilty, for allowing those four to dominate. We were all tainted by them.

And it was endless. It made a normal Musical Appreciation lesson seem like a hundred yard dash; this was the real thing, this was the marathon. Nobody knew where to look, what to do – to smile nervously, to look ashamed. I longed to run out of the room. Miss Pindock probably wouldn't even have noticed; she was too far gone for that. But I stuck it out. And above everything, all the time, the ceaseless, tuneless, howling row from the speakers.

42

"And now!" said Lisa Hennessey brightly, "for the Grand Finale!" There was a general ripple of indifference; it couldn't be worse than what had gone before. There was no response from Miss Pindock, huddled deep into her chair, a semi-comatose wraith. "'God Save the Queen,'" Lisa said triumphantly, "by the Malignant Diseases!" Sharply, as to a pre-arranged signal, Alison, Marie and Jennifer shot to their feet, and stood firmly to attention while the Diseases drawled their unpleasant way through their ghastly interpretation of the National Anthem. It was a travesty — the final farce. This did evoke a reaction from Miss Pindock; she gave a jerk, as if someone had stabbed her in the back.

The bell rang. Never have I seen a room empty so quickly. Tin and I were among the first through the door, so we never saw what happened: if there was any confrontation between Miss Pindock and Lisa. I think probably there wasn't. We waited in the corridor until Lisa emerged, complete with records and giggling retinue.

"Narf off, Chink," Lisa snapped, as soon as she saw Tin.

"You halfwit," said Tin. "You stupid, idiotic..."

"Narf off. Serves the old bitch right. Now she knows what it's been like for us all these years."

"Old cow," said Alison. "Taking my magazine. It's the nearest she's ever got to romance in her life. No man's ever been within a mile of her. Old cow."

Tin watched in silence as they walked away. Finally she said: "They dragged us all down to their level. That's why I'm so mad."

I remembered those four insolent faces, standing up at the end of the lesson, enjoying themselves at the expense of everyone else. "Next year," I said, "it's going to be different. Somehow. Those four aren't going to go on like this any longer."

"And what are *we* going to do about it?" Tin said bitterly.

"I don't think it'll be just us," I said. "Not after this."

Tin considered for a moment. "You know," she said, "I've just remembered the look on Margaret Dyson's face. I think you may be right. Sarah?"

"Mmm?"

"I think we ought to go back. Just to see if she's all right. Miss Pindock. She did look so odd."

"Oh – yes. I suppose." I knew what we'd find. She'd be sitting, motionless, clutching the boxed set of Beethoven, and, quite possibly, crying. What on earth could *we* do or say to make it any different? I didn't want to go back at all. But Tin was determined. We slunk to the door.

I was wrong. As we peered through the crack, what met our eyes was a flurry of action. There were little pink dots in Miss Pindock's cheeks, and her expression was not one of sorrow, but of a terrible anger. She was cleaning. She had a duster and a cloth and she was furiously, vigorously wiping all the dirt from her record player, wiping every last trace of the Damned and the Vermin from the turntables, the pickup, the stylus. She was exorcising the Exorcists.

"*Well*," whispered Tin, her face alight with admiration. "Look at that."

"She's tougher than I thought," I muttered.

"She'd have to be," said Tin, "to have put up with people like us all these years, and survived."

"I don't think we're necessary," I said; Tin nodded, and we crept away.

SALMONELLA

"Julia, it's twenty-five to eight," called Mrs. Rice. "You'll miss your bus!" She sounded as if this would rather please her; it would serve Julia right for getting up so late, for her stubborn refusal to rise at seven and thereby allow her mother sufficient time to fill her with a nice hot breakfast, before she set out into the cold and frosty morning. If Julia did miss that bus she wouldn't hear the end of it for a month. "Julia? Did you hear me?"

"*Yes*," said Julia, who was in the bathroom grappling with her tie. Beastly thing. There was a knack to tying ties, and Julia hadn't got it. The knot went too small, or if it was the right size it would end up somewhere near the second button down of her blouse; or if by some miracle she got both the size and the position right, one end would be a little stub of about two inches, while the other would be dangling somewhere round her knees. This was what had happened today. She was still half asleep, which didn't help. And before she could get out of the house her mother always looked at the tie – a look not so much of inspection as of comment, ah, I see you still haven't learned to knot your tie. Julia pulled on her jumper, which hid the worst of the damage, and went downstairs.

45

There was a strong and delicious aroma of frying bacon. Mrs. Rice had taken to doing bacon nearly every morning, since the start of what Julia secretly called the Breakfast War. Julia's mouth watered; the smell was cruelly lovely, but she wasn't to be beaten by low, underhand tactics like that. She hadn't *wanted* to go to Compton Park School, forty minutes away by bus, and only one possible bus. She'd wanted to go to Pringle Vale, where everyone she knew from junior school had gone; it was hardly any distance, and they didn't wear uniform there either, no stupid ties. She'd hang herself with that tie some day, a maroon and silver striped noose. It was the only sensible use for it. She hated ties, she hated Compton Park and she wasn't getting up at seven o'clock. The Breakfast War was about a good deal more than just breakfast.

Mrs. Rice came out from the kitchen into the hall. Julia turned away to get her coat, but not before her mother had glanced, knowingly, at the tie.

"It's twenty to," said Mrs. Rice, opening the front door. In came a blast of cold early-morning mid-October air. Julia shivered involuntarily. Her stomach was alerting her to its empty condition by means of a series of insistent rumbles. She felt terrible. "Hurry up," said her mother. "We don't all want to freeze to death, thank you." She said no more than this, but Julia could see, as if in a cartoon bubble over her mother's head, the words: "Going out on a morning like this with nothing hot inside you. And you with your weak chest. I doubt if you'll survive the winter."

And if I don't, replied Julia, making bubbles of her own, it'll be your fault, for making me go to Compton Park. She marched out into the bleak grey morning, ghostly under the half-light sky. The door was pulled firmly shut; her mother closing herself into the warm – warm, breakfast, *bacon* ... no, she wouldn't, she wouldn't care. It was the first time she'd ever consistently defied her mother about anything. If she gave in now she'd lose much, much more than she'd gained. She mustn't give in. In three hours it would be Break and she could get something to eat. *Food...*

As she plodded towards Avenue Road and the bus stop the usual two thoughts were running through Julia's mind. One: what if the bus goes five minutes early and I miss it? Two: is the girl there yet? Missing the bus was a constant anxiety. Once in Avenue Road she would be safe – the stop was only fifteen yards round the corner, she would see the bus coming and she could run for it. Here in Beech Lane she was helpless. At any moment the bus might thunder past the junction, huge monster, green and brightly lit ... every single morning, she lived this through in her mind. She quickened her step, eyes fixed on Avenue Road ahead. What if she did miss it? Go back home? *No.* Stand for three-quarters of an hour at the stop until the next one came – and then it would be midway through the first lesson when she got to school, and there'd be trouble. She'd never missed it yet, admittedly, but that didn't mean much; it had been only five weeks and there were years and years ahead – seven years of possible missed buses and dawn panics and Breakfast War. She wondered if the girl had ever missed the bus.

And here was Avenue Road, four people at the bus stop and no bus in sight. And, better and better, the last in the queue was the girl. Julia hurried the last few yards to the stop, in case some other queuer might materialize and beat her to it – and slipped into place. Directly behind her. The very best position, for close observation. Perhaps it would be a good day after all.

Julia had noticed the girl on the very first day; she hadn't expected that anyone else might be going to Compton Park from her stop. For the first week or so she'd just seen her as a maroon blazer and skirt with a body inside. Her dislike of the dreaded uniform had been the strongest thing. But then

47

she began to be interested. She saw the girl's face, and it was a most fascinating face, healthy and cheeky and mischievous, the sort of face that looks to be for ever on the point of breaking into a broad grin. Julia had seen her grin once, at someone walking past the bus stop. It was, as grins go, a smasher. Her skin was smooth and beautiful, with a scattering of freckles on the uptilted nose. Her hair was short, straight, a rich thick chestnutty-brown. And there was something about the combination of these elements that Julia found unnervingly haunting.

And now she was standing just nine inches behind this person. It was a very privileged feeling. Julia had spun such a web of fantasy around the girl. She had given her a personality, a family – if only she knew her name! – and here she was, nose-to-blazer with the reality. She *would* have a blazer. Julia longed for a blazer instead of the awful coat. Even the smallest size of Compton Park coat had been masses too big for her, but "you'll grow into it," said her mother as usual. Julia sometimes felt that her entire life had been spent attempting to grow into clothes, and failing.

There was still no sign of the bus. *Stay away*, Julia told it, wanting despite the cold to prolong these precious moments, although all she could see of the girl was her satchel, and a great deal of back. *Be late*. Defiantly the bus appeared in the distance – just an arrangement of lights, but the queue knew it for what it was and began to rustle, press forward, fumble for fares. It was astonishing how quickly you acquired talents like identifying a 407 bus a quarter of a mile away on a dark morning. Winter drawing in, good. Julia felt happy just at the thought of it. She loved the winter, snow and ice and frost and glowering dramatic gloomy skies. She loved coming indoors out of the cold and warming herself by the fire. Summer heat gave her headaches, summer sun burned and peeled her. She was definitely a winter person, she thought with satisfaction, glad of any identity, any definition of herself.

The bus drew to a halt, brakes shuddering, engine turning. As always it was nearly empty. The girl went to her usual seat, downstairs, at the front, right-hand side. Julia had at first travelled upstairs, because she liked the view, but now, of course, she wouldn't dream of it; she had selected a regular downstairs seat of her own, one of the sideways ones at the back. These were raised higher than the forward-facing ones, so she could see everything (including the girl). She sat at the back of the classroom for the same reason: to see, rather than be seen. It made her feel less vulnerable.

If *only* I knew her name, thought Julia for the millionth time as the bus pulled out. All she knew, really, was that the girl lived down Broadmeadow Road or one of the turnings off it, and that she must be thirteen years old. In the beginning Julia had assumed she was a fifth former at least – she seemed so tall, so grown-up – but then Julia was so very small. Almost everyone at Compton Park seemed, to her, older than they could possibly be. The sixth formers! She hadn't dared to speak to one yet. She never could. She'd have thought them all teachers if it hadn't been for the uniform.

She'd found out the girl's form quite by accident. Julia's class had been coming out of room 25 after the last lesson of the day, and as she'd passed room 24 Julia had seen the girl go inside, and open a desk. So that must be her formroom. It was the work of a moment to look at the chart in the entrance hall and discover that 24 was 3T's room. A Third Year! Only two years' difference between them! This narrowing of the gulf was enormously heartening.

But it hadn't got her anywhere, had it? They'd never so much as said "Hi." And Julia couldn't – *couldn't* bring herself to break the ice. She was terrified of talking to strangers. Her whole body froze up; her stomach turned to

49

lead and ice. She'd always been the same. She would rehearse opening gambits, friendly remarks, and sometimes for a while even believe that she was the sort of person who could say them. Like her mother, who struck up conversations effortlessly on buses, trains, in queues, in waiting rooms, without even seeming to think about it. Her mother would have been great friends with the girl by now. She'd have been up there, sharing that front seat with her, chatting away. Whereas, here was Julia, on her own. As usual. With so much to say, and nobody, nobody to say it to. Nothing was any different; nothing would ever change. Miserably she dug around in her satchel, found her French book and began to go through the vocabulary which she knew already, for Julia was such a *good* girl, and always did her homework thoroughly; for no other reason than that she was terrified of the consequences if she didn't.

Soon the French blurred, and Julia drifted into conversation with the girl. They discussed the school play (the girl thought Julia ought to try for a part; no, no, said Julia, she couldn't possibly, she wouldn't stand a chance); they talked about the Breakfast War ("I think you're quite right to stick to your guns," said the girl) – about the girl's younger brother and sister ("they're an awful nuisance, but I'm quite fond of them, really. You must come round and meet them sometime...") – and suddenly Julia awoke from the dream with a startled jerk, for there was the girl passing her, getting off – they must have reached the school stop, and she hadn't noticed. The girl hoisted her satchel on to her shoulder; Julia got up and followed her out – and there, she saw what had been invisible in the semi-dark at the bus stop. On the flap of the satchel, in tiny black letters, was inked – Julia blinked, scarcely able to believe in this unexpected good fortune, this gift from a kindly god – was inked a name, and then a form: the form, as she knew, was 3T. The name was S. Wilder.

Wilder, Wilder, Wilder. It ran singing through her head, across the asphalt, into the school building, up to her formroom, down to Assembly. Wilder. It was *beautiful*. How lucky – it might have been Higginbotham. But *Wilder*. S. S is for – what? Susan, Samantha, Sharon, she thought, through hymn, prayers, announcements, back up to the formroom, along to room 16 for English. S for what? Sheila – possible, it suited her. Stephanie too. Shelley – oh please not Shelley, Shelley Wilder sounded too – too wobbly. Sadie, Suzanne, Stella. Sian – yes, that would do. Sally, Selina, Sylvia. None of those. *Scarlett*, she thought, straying happily into the realms of the fantastical – Sabrina, Soraya, Salmonella – no! That was poison!

Why, oh why, couldn't she, Julia, have a name like Wilder? Instead of beastly Rice, stupid name, long grain short grain or patna. And of course, there would be, there just *would* be a boy in her form called Daniel Curry. The rest of them – clever dicks – hadn't been exactly slow to notice this, and start in with their awful embarrassing jokes. Just because she was unlucky enough to be lumbered with a rotten boring name like...

"Julia Rice!"

"Pardon ... yes, Mrs. Dempsey?"

"Do me the courtesy of paying attention, if you don't mind, Julia."

"Yes, Mrs. Dempsey." Julia flushed pink. Everyone turned round to have a look; rare sight, that, Julia Rice getting told off. With most other offenders Mrs. Dempsey would have gone on to give them a proper roasting, but Julia was such a good girl and so hard-working; it was clearly only a momentary lapse, and unlikely to be repeated. Julia sighed. She did so hate being good. She *longed* to be bad. But Julia had been brought up to know that the sole purpose of her existence, as a child, was to please adults, and to earn their approval. And now, when she was

51

finally coming to doubt this knowledge, it was too late. She was too set in her ways to alter them – or too cowardly. She didn't know how to be bad. Yet, if she was what they all thought her to be, why these subversive thoughts? What was the real Julia Rice? *Was* there a real Julia Rice?

Break finally arrived, and Julia hurried to silence her hunger pangs. There was a choice; you could rush for the snacks queue, or rush for the drinks machine queue. Either way you stood no chance of getting to the front of the other. Julia opted for the snacks, though she yearned terribly for hot, milky sweet coffee. Her mother could have provided her with a flask of coffee, but of course she refused to do this. "If you want coffee you can drink it at the breakfast table like any civilized human being." So – crisps and biscuits.

"*Outside* unless you're queueing!" roared the prefects, strutting about officiously. They would send you out into anything short of a blizzard. Julia stood outside, munched and shivered. She was alone. She was always alone. All the other First Years had come from just a few local junior schools – everybody knew somebody and already, in the fifth week of term, friendship patterns had been established, friendships which in no way threatened to involve Julia. It was only what she'd expected. She didn't brood on it. She was too occupied with thinking of S-names.

She couldn't carry on wondering like this. She had to know, and the only way to find out was to go up to room 24, when it was empty, and look at the lists on the form noticeboard. She'd go today, after school. It would only take a moment, and then – she hugged herself, anticipating the glorious discovery – she would *know*. Although she had already decided that it would almost certainly be Sarah. Not exactly exotic, but somehow right. There is a certain Sarah face, and the girl had it, a very superior specimen, but the right type.

The day passed without further event. The only bad

thing was games – Julia loathed all lessons like games and cookery and drama. She had no confidence for these moving-about lessons where you weren't safely behind a desk for the entire forty minutes. After school she waited ten minutes – surely that was long enough for a formroom to clear – and then made her way upstairs, trying hard to look purposeful, to acquire the expression of someone who has a legitimate reason for her journey.

Not that anyone took the slightest notice of her. Room 24 was on the second floor, midway along a corridor with a staircase at each end. Escape routes, she thought nervously, approaching the door – what would she say, now, if someone came out and asked what she was doing here? What ...

The room was empty. Silently she slipped through the door. There was the noticeboard, and a list with the names of 3T, in alphabetical order. With a massive effort of will, she forced herself to look down slowly from the top, savouring the moment ... Thomas – Walker – Weston – Wilder.

Sheridan Wilder.

Sheridan. It was too much. It was too perfect. Sheridan! She skipped to the door, made to turn right, had a fleeting impression of people approaching from the far end of the corridor, swung to the left, heart galloping, and bounded down the stairs, heart galloping. Sheridan Wilder.

Her thoughts on the bus home made the old ones seem very drab: black and white outlines. Now she could fill in the colours, a whole rainbow of detail. The younger brother and sister, previously nameless, became Ashley and Kimberley. They would look much like Sheridan – it was a face which would, with minor adjustments, do equally well for a boy or a girl. Little Kimberley would be a sweet, adorable miniature Sheridan. The parents – artistic sort of people, obviously. She would love the whole family. She ...

But she still had never spoken to Sheridan. It was ridiculous. The two of them on this bus, eighty minutes a day, five days a week; it was obviously *meant* that they should be friends. There was nothing more Julia could ask from life than to have Sheridan Wilder for a friend. But yet – there was Sheridan at the front, and here was Julia at the back. All the wonderful conversations they should be having! She must speak to her. Perhaps tomorrow morning she'd summon up the courage from somewhere. She *must*. But what to say? Well, there were hours ahead to think of that.

There was a red car parked outside the Rices' house. Right in front of the gate. Cheek! Dad would be furious. But then, as she got closer, the car began to look familiar. Oh, hell. Liz. Her mother's ghastly friend Liz. Julia was supposed to call her Auntie Liz, but that seemed so childish, so stupid, when she *wasn't* an aunt, that Julia avoided calling her anything at all. Trust Liz to choose a good day like this to spoil.

"*Hello*, dear," said Liz, gush gush, as Julia came in.

"Hello."

"Really, Julia," said her mother, "I don't know what's happening to your manners. Auntie Liz has a name. Hello, Auntie Liz."

"Hello, *Auntie* Liz," said Julia tightly, stressing the "Auntie" bit as if to emphasize the ridiculousness of it.

"You'll have to excuse Julia," said Mrs. Rice, her eyes flashing ten degrees of frost. "She seems to have forgotten how to behave." "I'll deal with you later," floated up in a bubble.

"Oh, it's *quite* all right," said Liz graciously, giving Julia a smile of sweet understanding. Julia stood there, hating her. "I know. These difficult little phases. They all go through them. How are you settling at Compton Park, dear? Are you making friends?"

"She never seems to make friends," said her mother. "She finds it *very* difficult. I've never understood it. It must be that she doesn't make the effort."

"I'm settling in all right, thanks," said Julia, as if her mother hadn't spoken. Somehow, almost being friends with Sheridan was giving her a daring and confidence she'd never before possessed. "Considering that it's so far away, and that I never wanted to go there at all."

"*Here* we go," said Mrs. Rice with a long-suffering sigh. She and Liz exchanged glances; it was apparent that Liz had already been told all about the Breakfast War. "I think you'd better go upstairs and start your homework, Julia. I'll call you when tea's ready."

"All right."

"All right who?"

Count Dracula. Jack the Ripper. Attila the Hun. "All right, Mum."

Liz stayed for tea, and seemed set fair to stay all evening, making herself comfortable in Julia's armchair. Julia decided to have a lot of homework to do that night; she'd go upstairs again as soon as possible. She had to stay down for a while, to see her father. It was expected. Because these days Julia had left the house before he got up in the mornings. So they sat, and saw each other, Julia uncomfortable in a straight-backed chair, her father dozing. It was all very thrilling. Liz was reading the evening paper, Mrs. Rice watching the television.

Julia wriggled and squirmed, gazed blankly at the screen, at her father's slippered feet, at the wall, at the back of Liz's paper, at the floor – then did a double take and looked back at the paper. SHYNESS—THE AGONY said the headline. And underneath: 'Do you find it impossible to make conversation with strangers?' It might as well have said: "Is your name Julia Rice?" – Julia gave a self-conscious start

55

and quickly averted her eyes, trying not to appear interested, though it was probably too late – they had seen, they were all scanning the headline and thinking: "Ah, Julia. That would seem to apply to you." And then Liz would read the whole item out and they'd all sit there gazing at her, knowingly. She couldn't bear it.

There was a crackling, an unmistakable crackling. Julia lifted her eyes momentarily – yes, incredibly, Liz had folded the paper and was putting it aside. She was saved! But – she wouldn't mind reading the article herself, as long as nobody knew. She *needed* to read it! It was probably full of answers – it would tell her what to do, what to say – she *had* to see it. But it was Liz's paper. There was no way in the world she could read Liz's paper without their knowing, and then they'd flip through to see what could possibly have interested Julia so much ... "Oh, *look*, Liz." "What, Marion?" "Shyness. Well of course. Well this is absolutely Julia. Listen to this..."

She'd just have to go out and buy a copy of her own.

"Julia? Where are you going?"

"To the newsagent's. It's still open."

"The newsagent's? Whatever do you want from there, at this time of night?"

"Chocolate," said Julia desperately.

"Chocolate? There's chocolate in the fridge."

"What sort?"

"Oh, I don't know ... Galaxy, I think."

"I wanted a Flake," said Julia, thrusting her arms into her coat sleeves.

"Well, don't be long. It's dark. You shouldn't be out on your own after dark. Chocolate, indeed. You've just eaten a good tea. You shouldn't be hungry. Of course it's well known that if you skip breakfast you're hungry for the rest of the day."

"Chocolate's so bad for the skin," said Liz happily.

Julia bought the paper and a Flake as well; she could quite imagine her mother demanding to see it. She hid the paper carefully inside her coat. Even the hated coat had its uses.

"I'm back," she shouted, closing the front door firmly behind her, and hurried upstairs without further elaboration. She stood a chair against her bedroom door. It wouldn't keep anybody out, but it should give her enough time to stuff the paper under her bed. If only her mother would knock, instead of barging straight in. But: "Knock on doors in my own house? Only servants knock."

Hungrily she read the article, with an uncomfortable sensation of furtive guilt – it was too close, it had spilled her open, it was *her*, her inner self in print for all to see in the *Gazette*. But her unease was less than her fascination. She went back and read it again. Certain sentences and phrases seemed to stand out:

"For the truly shy person, shyness is a constant burden which torments them daily ... Shy people are almost totally wrapped up in themselves and have a very low opinion of their worth. Normal contact with hitherto unknown people is for the shy person an ordeal of terrifying dimensions. They live in constant fear of ridicule and rejection. Their apparent coldness is often misinterpreted. In fact, the shy person is yearning to make friends, but this yearning is never quite so strong as the need to protect themselves from possible injury to their fragile self-esteem."

Well, it made sense. But – oh dear, it was so very unflattering. Yet, according to the article, which was by a psychologist, there were millions of other people miserably battling with the same shameful problem.

"Does it ever occur to you that other people may be shy too? That the very person you're longing to get to know is probably suffering from the same communication-handicap as you?" That made it sound almost respectable. Oh no,

I'm not shy, goodness me no, I just have this communication-handicap.

"The other person is almost certainly wondering why *you* don't like *them* enough to speak! A great deal of needless soul-searching goes on; neither party suspects the other of being shy. So – take your courage in your hands, and break the ice with a friendly, casual remark. It's never quite so hard as you think! Your advances will almost certainly be welcomed with great relief! Beat shyness – the rewards are tremendous. Don't let it beat you!"

Wondering, she laid the paper aside. It was all *so* true. It *hadn't* ever occurred to her that Sheridan was shy too. She did only think of herself. And yet, it was now so obvious. It was something they'd have in common; they could help each other to overcome it. But she, Julia, would have to be the brave one, the one to make that dreaded first move, because Sheridan wouldn't have read the article. Sheridan did not understand the situation.

Or perhaps she *had* read it, and was at this moment thinking the same things about Julia. It would be so funny, if tomorrow morning they both turned to each other and began to talk at the same time. What would she say? She lay back on the bed, going through her (unused) repertoire of opening remarks. Nothing seemed quite right. She was still thinking about it when she settled down for the night, and was soon in the throes of a dream where she was sitting with little Kimberley on her lap and all the other Wilders around her – Mrs. Wilder was handing out Flakes (she looked just like Sheridan) – the walls of the Wilder sitting-room were covered with portraits of the children, painted by their parents, in repeating patterns like wallpaper – suddenly the room began to shake and rattle, and it had turned into the bus. Julia began to be worried because she hadn't got her satchel with her and there would be terrible trouble when she got to school – "you can have mine," said Mrs. Wilder –

rattle rattle, and now the bus was shaking more violently, it was shaking her, shaking...

"Julia. It's quarter past seven," said Mrs. Rice, shaking Julia's shoulder firmly. "You must get up! You'll miss your bus!"

"Oh, no!" said Julia, sitting bolt upright, looking out of the window at the blue-grey – the half-light seemed exciting, atmospheric on this magical morning. "I'm *up*, look."

"What's got into *you* this morning?" said Mrs. Rice, never satisfied, and left the room with a sniff.

Everything was right. Even the tie consented to be knotted rather more elegantly than usual. Her reflection in the mirror was, almost, pretty – perhaps because she was smiling. She would smile more often. She didn't even worry about the bus being early, as she walked eagerly down Beech Lane – it wouldn't do that to her, today. Round the corner into Avenue Road – and there was Sheridan. As usual, the sight of the flesh-and-blood Sheridan, after so many hours with the imaginary one, made her insides lurch. Come on, Julia. Forget the nerves. Rise above them. It's easier than you think, remember. *Do* it!

"Excuse me." Nothing. No reaction. She didn't look round – oh help...

"Excuse me – have you ever missed the bus?" Oh, why did it sound so feeble? Why was her voice so strange, so scared and small? Why couldn't it sound friendly and casual like the article said?

Slowly, Sheridan Wilder turned her head.

"Huh?"

"I said, have you ever missed the bus?" She'd done it! She was talking to Sheridan – and it hadn't been so difficult, had it? She'd broken the block. After all these years. She could talk to strangers.

Sheridan hadn't said anything. She was just standing

there looking at Julia, expressionless, blank. Finally she gave the ghost of a grin, her marvellous grin, and said:

"You know the bus stop up there at the end of Alexandra Road?"

"Yes!" said Julia eagerly. As easy as this. They were talking about buses. The obvious thing.

"How long'd it take you to get there, from your house?"

"Oh, not that long – I'd go down Briar Way and turn left – I live in Beech Lane, you know – I suppose about ten minutes."

"Good. Then I bleedin' well wish you'd start out five minutes earlier and wait for the bus up there, instead of standing here gawping at me every morning like something from the nuthouse. Bloody little creep. You think we haven't seen you hanging round outside our formroom? You're a great joke in our form. We call you the Moron. And what were you doing in our room after school last night, eh? *We* saw you. Little creep. Just sod off, will you?"

Later, what seemed so remarkable to Julia was not the words Sheridan used but the voice with which she spoke them. She hadn't heard Sheridan speak before. Her voice was rough and coarse and ugly and what her mother would call "studying to be a fishwife". Julia couldn't have known. She'd been cruelly deceived by the face – that face! – and the treacherous name. The shock of the voice, in time, almost obliterated the shock of the words. She'd been too stunned to take them in fully, and her memory was kind, and didn't hold on to them with its normal tenacity. But this was when the rawness of the pain had eased to a dull ache, only occasionally interrupted by an agonizing, stabbing spasm of hurt. When she could think of it without tears smarting in her eyes. Much, much later.

"Might I ask," said Mrs. Rice, "Why you've taken to leaving the house at half past seven, now?"

"I go to the Alexandra Road stop," Julia said stiffly.

"Oh. Might I ask why?"

You have asked, haven't you? "It's – there's this girl – at the other stop – I can't get on with her – I thought it would be best."

"Oh, *Julia*. The same old story. What *is* it about you that puts people's backs up? You *won't* get on with people. You won't make the effort. *Did* you make the effort?"

"No," said Julia.

"Who is this girl? What's her name?"

Julia clenched her teeth, and said: "Salmonella Wilder."

"Salmonella – oh, really, Julia, do you have to be so ridiculous? What is the matter with you these days? You can't have a sensible conversation . . . salmonella is a sort of bacteria. It gives you food poisoning."

"Poison," said Julia, nodding. Her mother released a massive sigh of long-accumulated impatience, and continued to unpack her shopping bag. "Jelly," she murmured, "beans, oranges – waffles. I thought your father and I might try waffles for breakfast. So delicious, with maple syrup. But of course, you won't be joining us."

"All right," said Julia indifferently.

"I beg your pardon?"

"I said all right. I'll get up for breakfast."

"Well, there's a good girl! I knew all along that you'd see sense in the end. You'll find, you know, that I'm generally right about these things."

It didn't matter any more. She would always lose; she would always be the same. Nothing would change. And it just wasn't worth fighting any more. She was nothing.

"Good girl," said her mother.

THE BLACK SHEEP

Russell Archer glanced at the blinking green digits of his Individual Multi-Purpose unit. The IMP was a stereo radio cassette television calculator alarm clock, with inbuilt personal computer. It also made tea and toast, but Russell rarely availed himself of these facilities; for some time now he had been living on raspberry jelly, milk chocolate and unsweetened apple juice. Russell had a complex and tortuous relationship with his IMP. He hated it; he despised its very microcircuits; frequently he longed to hurl it out of the window. But somehow he could never bring himself to harm it in any way – the loss of the IMP would leave an unfillable void in his life. If, thought Russell, you could call it a life. What was life anyway? Why was life? Why not? Who cared?

21.59, said the green digits. It was nearly time. Russell switched the radio on. He supposed it was better to know the worst. He could just as well have used the television, but Russell had great difficulty, these days, in coping with heavy visual experiences. He never put the light on except to do his homework; otherwise he sat in the dark, with the room illuminated only by the ghostly green figures of the IMP, and brooded on the meaning of his existence, and the general futility of everything. "Peep, peep, blip," said the radio. "It's ten o'clock; here is the news. Ten minutes ago in the House of Commons the Government was defeated in the vote of confidence by two votes. A General Election is now expected at the end of May. Here is how the House heard the news..."

It was all he needed to know. Russell groaned heavily, and switched the radio off, accidentally activating the IMP's Talk button. "Gee, Russell, you're a nice person," said the IMP. Russell yelped and flipped it to Silence. So that was that, then. A General Election.

Not for the first time, Russell yearned to be somebody else. Somebody who could ignore the election; somebody who was not the son of the sitting M.P. of his constituency. From now until election day their house would be chaos. There would be agents, photographers, campaign organizers, secretaries, reporters – total madness. Russell would have hated it at the best of times, but *now*, with his exams coming up in June, and his Maths so totally hopeless, and needing five passes – as if all that wasn't enough. Perhaps he'd be able to use the exams as an excuse. Perhaps he could shut himself away up here in his room, with an endless supply of juice and jelly and chocolate, and not emerge until the whole frightful thing was over. If it wasn't for having to go to school he'd do just that. An election. It was too unspeakably awful. He threw a blanket over the IMP, and fell into a depressed sort of sleep.

Russell wasn't good at mornings. The next day he stumbled downstairs, dozily and blearily, at ten to eight. The IMP had woken him at seven thirty with a loud bleeping and a vile cheerful cry of: "Wakey wakey, Russell! It's the start of a wonderful new day! Aren't you just glad to be alive?" ... and then, five minutes later: "Russell, I have to warn you that if you aren't up in three minutes I shall be forced to turn on my siren..." Russell lurched into the kitchen to be greeted by the awful sight of brilliant daylight, and his father, brother and sister seated round the table looking absolutely foul: clean and bright and sparkly, and gobbling away like something out of a breakfast cereal commercial.

"What a disgusting sight," said his father, meaning Russell. Russell didn't argue the point. "Have those socks *ever* been washed, do you think?"

"Dunno," said Russell, trying to remember if he'd slept in them. He tottered sleepily to the fridge, and found a half-eaten dish of raspberry jelly. He took this to the table.

"You aren't still eating that, are you?" said Marcus, spooning away virtuously at his muesli. Marcus was twelve. "It's unhealthy, what you eat. You don't get any fibre at all. You'll make yourself ill, you will. You'll probably get diverticular disease," he said happily, "and chronic constipation."

"Shuddup and eat your oats," said Russell, contemplating the jelly.

"What's diverticular?" asked Tonia.

"We don't wish to know," said their father, buttering wholemeal toast. Russell decided he couldn't face the jelly. Perhaps he was going off it. Gloomily he sat and sipped apple juice.

"I suppose you heard the news last night?" said Mr. Archer.

"Oh, that. Yeah."

"Your mother rang. The House was sitting till very late, so she spent the night in London. She'll be back about two, she said."

"Oh good," said Tonia, who was ten, and a great public relations asset.

"And then," continued her father, "all hell will be let loose. Thanks to the boundary changes Eve's been made

64

into a Key Marginal. That means all the usual hullabaloo doubled. If not tripled."

"I can't bear it," said Russell. "I've got my exams coming up."

"You've no choice. Television cameras everywhere, there'll be, and straw polls and the Press. The media will descend in their millions."

"I like being on TV," said Marcus. "Is Mum going to lose her seat then, or what?"

"Well, it's possible. Very possible. There's almost certain to be a swing, you see, against the Government. And the United Party have got a strong candidate in our constituency. It's likely to be a very close thing. That," he added, "is why it's called a Marginal."

Russell blinked. He'd forgotten all about the boundary changes. So she might lose, might she? He could sum up no more enthusiasm for her defeat than he could for her victory. Being an M.P. kept her so very busy. Kept her out of the house. She was always organizing something, his mother – at least when she was in Parliament she didn't have so much time to organize him. "Look lively, Russell! . . . Come along, Russell, join in, darling!" Ugh.

Russell wasn't into party politics. He was very heavily out of them. In his experience it made little difference whether his mother's party, the Democrats, or the other lot, the United Party, were in power. Things went on just the same; sooner or later there was an election, the teams changed sides and off they went again. Russell doubted if he'd ever vote for either of them. The only party he was in any sympathy with was the Apathy Party, and it was well known that the Apathy Party were never able to summon up the energy or the interest to put up any candidates. In the Great General Election of Life, I am a permanent abstainer, thought Russell, dazzled by the profundity of this notion.

Russell had a terrible day at school. In his Maths set there was a boy called Dean, ebullient, loud-mouthed and a great supporter of the United Party. "I see your ma's gonna be joining my dad on the dole, Archer," he said as soon as Russell arrived.

"Your dad's not on the dole," said Russell.

"No thanks to your ma," said Dean, "and her rotten Government's policies."

You couldn't win. It wasn't *her* Government; she wasn't even in the Cabinet, though she had been tipped as a possible Junior Minister in the next reshuffle. But Dean blamed Russell's mother for everything. When he failed a Maths test he put it down to her odious influence on the Minister of Education, whom, Dean claimed, she was constantly leading astray. It was unforunate that the Minister of Education was called Adam, and Russell's mother, Eve.

And it went on all day. Every teacher, it seemed, had his or her own particular little quip. He was pointed out to First Years as he shambled down the corridors, trying to look anonymous. This was the worst single thing about having a parent in Parliament. Everybody *knew*. Although Russell, being a boy, had taken his father's, not his mother's surname, they knew just the same. "Russell Archer? Oh yes, Eve Carroll's son." Every time she appeared on television, or was featured in the local paper, the wisecrackers would be waiting for him, next day. And – it was still painful to think of – the time she'd made that great long speech about sex education being the responsibility of the family – well, Russell had just about died with the embarrassment of it. He'd hung his head for weeks; his face had done the whole range from palest rose to full blast beetroot, again and again.

Russell was deeply thoughtful as he slouched home that

evening. There did seem to be a pretty good case to be made for wanting his mother to lose. One last final round of teasing and the jibes would cease for ever. Or would they? There was the catch. Would she retire gracefully from public life to become a Full Time Parent? Not her. She'd simply zap off in another direction. Probably she'd get herself a TV chat show and be on every single *week*. Russell shuddered.

At this point he remembered a more urgent problem: the page of algebra in his bag awaiting his dubious attentions – algebra that must be handed in tomorrow morning. He stopped and bought twelve Moons of Saturn to sustain him. These were little chocolate globes, four inches in diameter, their surfaces pitted with craters, their insides any one of a variety of unearthly fillings. Russell chewed dolorously through a Titan as he plodded up to his front door.

The garden was full of people. "Oh, it's Russell," said somebody, without noticeable enthusiasm. His mother was there and his father; Marcus and Tonia, looking suspiciously tidy; Sandy Coppard, standing in the centre of the room and issuing orders; two other women, visible through the French window, were pacing in the back garden, while, in a corner, looking out of things, was a little man, busily writing.

"Russell," said his mother, swooping over in a welcoming sort of way. Eve Carroll was small, curly-haired and bouncy; a bubbling energetic human dynamo. Russell could never understand how he had come to inherit half his genes from such a person. "How are you, darling?"

"Depressed," said Russell.

"Still the same old Russell," said Sandy Coppard, with obvious regret. Sandy was his mother's media agent. She was impossibly successful. Her other clients included the England cricket captain, four disc jockeys, three newscasters, a rising snooker star and the Chancellor of the Exchequer. Russell loathed her.

"Can we do the photographs now?" asked Tonia, kicking her heels with impatience. Tonia was wearing a T-shirt that said: TONIA CARROLL: YOUR NEXT PRIME MINISTER BUT FIVE.

"What's going on?" asked Russell. "Who are *they*?" He nodded at the meandering women, and at the little man in the corner.

"The ladies are photographers," said his mother. "Sandy brought them. And this gentleman's a reporter from the *Chorwell Journal*. He's doing an On the Spot Profile, isn't that right, Mr. Um, Er..."

"Don't mind me," said the man, feverishly scribbling, and shrinking further back into his chair.

"We're getting some new photos done for the campaign," Sandy said, briskly. "The Candidate as Caring Parent; posed in the Candidate's garden, with her children. Children could be a very important factor in Eve's victory. The United Party candidate has one son only, and he's a glue-sniffer. Come on, everyone. Out you go."

"What!" said Russell, appalled. "You mean *me*?" Him, with a great shiny spot on his face which would glow like a beacon in the afternoon sun; with his stupid long arms and his awful nose which had taken on a vigorous life of its own, lately; his hair greasier than a chip pan with the dandruff billowing down in gusts...

"Maybe Russell has a point, there," said Sandy, scrutinizing him. "I wonder, Eve. Think back. At the last election Tonia was six, Marcus eight, Russell elevenish, all pre-adolescent, very charming. Now look. I mean, am I or am I not trying to project a youthful image for you, Eve? I mean, Eve, without wishing to denigrate Russell in any way, we have to face the fact that he has grown ... he may not be entirely..."

"I'm so ugly, I'd probably lose her votes," said Russell, and, turning, traipsed from the room.

"Russell!" cried his mother. "She didn't mean that at all – Russell, come back."

"I've a lot of work to do," said Russell, climbing the stairs. Nobody, he noticed, made much effort to stop him. He heard the French windows being opened, and his family being arranged to illustrate the Candidate as Caring Parent. Phoney, thought Russell wearily. Hypocrisy. Total crud. He pushed his bedroom door open. "Gee, Russell," said the IMP, its sensory device detecting his footsteps, "it's good to have you back here. I've got very positive feelings about you, Russ..."

"Oh shut up," said Russell, and flipped the silencer. The IMP gave a squawk of indignation and subsided.

Some four hours later, his mother came up and knocked on the door. "Russell? Do come downstairs, darling. I haven't *seen* you!"

"Haven't finished my homework," said Russell, who hadn't started it. He'd been lying flat on his back, munching Moons, meditating, trying to shut out the constant buzz of voices and ringing of the telephone downstairs, and to elevate himself to a higher mental plane.

"Russell. You're not to work any longer. You'll have a breakdown. You'll damage your eyesight. Come down and have something to eat."

Russell knew she would stay there, pestering and nagging, until he came. It was quicker to give in straight away. Oh, life was putrid.

His family were all in the living room. The others had gone. That was something.

"He's still got those socks on," said Marcus.

"Are you eating, Russell?"

"He's got half a jelly in the fridge," said Marcus. Russell glowered at him.

"I've gone off it," he said.

"Have some mousse, then," said Eve. "There's plenty

69

left. I think it's still in the garden room."

"No fibre in mousse," said Marcus, as Russell departed in a resigned sort of way. He was somewhat surprised to find, in the garden room, the little man from the *Journal*, still in his corner, and still writing. "Have I to go now?" asked the man, looking disappointed.

"You can stay there all night," said Russell, "as far as I'm concerned." He picked up the mousse and returned to the living room.

"Maria rang, Russell," said his mother. Trying to draw me into the conversation, thought Russell. Maria was the Prime Minister. "Apparently I'm even more marginal than they first realized, so they're sending down one of the big guns to help me out. I'm hoping for Elspeth, but it seems it may have to be Angus." Elspeth was the Minister for Sport; Angus the Chancellor of the Exchequer.

"Oh, well, that's brilliant, isn't it," said Mr. Archer. "He's only the most unpopular man in the country. If he turns up in Chorwell you'll probably lose your deposit."

"But I don't see how I can keep him away. One has to be tactful. Poor Angus," said Eve. "Sandy tries so hard to make the public love him. I suppose – with Angus – well, it's difficult." Sandy's efforts on behalf of the Chancellor were well known. Only this year she had persuaded him to publish a boxed set consisting of two volumes: *The Chancellor's Joke Book* and *The Joy of Budgeting*. The sole result of this was that the Chancellor's wax effigy in Madame Tussaud's was moved to the Chamber of Horrors, where he was regularly outpointing all the other residents in the Most Hated Character poll.

"Will people throw eggs at him, if he comes?" asked Tonia.

"I expect so," her mother said gloomily. "They always do. No – this isn't good enough. I am not going to fight this election in a negative frame of mind. We're all going to pull

70

together and march to a splendid and glorious victory. Right, everyone? Right, Russell?"

"This mousse is really disgusting," said Russell.

The media went berserk. It was a very poor year for Big Events; no Olympics, no World Cup, no Royal Occasion – not even a really juicy scandal, so far. While letter-boxes throughout the country rattled daily with the stream of literature sent out by the various parties, all the TV channels settled down to what amounted to saturation election coverage. Debates, personality profiles and opinion polls abounded; the experts proudly demonstrated their latest computers, which could illustrate, predict and compare Swings and Turnouts with newly stunning visual effect and at lightning speed. There was an Election Song Contest, and re-runs of the highlights of elections past.

Much attention was paid to the minority parties, who were busy mustering their troops in preparation for their regular gala of lost deposits. The Primal Scream Party caused much alarm with their public rallies in town centres; there were also the Divine Intervention Party, the Nearly Normal Party, and the much acclaimed All in the Mind Party, who held that if the public ceased to believe in politicians, the politicians would cease to exist. This hypothesis was debated on Panorama.

In Chorwell, the local papers had emerged as the central battlefield. Eve Carroll had been greatly startled when she came downstairs in the morning to find the little journalist still in his chair, and still writing, very pleased with his Nighttime Profile of the household. Eve, a practised diplomat, gave him a superb breakfast before sending him on his way; the resulting article in the Journal was fulsome in its praise of Eve and her entire family, saving only Russell, who was described as 'a strange and joyless youth'.

Sandy Coppard made a few innocent remarks in the right

71

places, and soon the whole gruesome tale of the United candidate's glue-sniffing son appeared under a banner headline. The United Party, however, countered this cleverly. Not only, they said, had the boy now taken the pledge and put aside the adhesive bottle for ever; he was doing a Duke of Edinburgh Award. They produced documentary evidence. Sandy was livid.

They were miserable days for Russell. His mother, admittedly, was rarely at home, but her place had been taken by the campaign army: in and out, at all hours, were Sandy, John, his mother's political agent, her secretary Arthur, her campaign manager Gillian, all rushing to and fro from local HQ, off to the next meeting place – it was unspeakably gruesome. Once Russell came in and found, in the garden room, fourteen thousand computer-written letters, and nineteen Young Democrats, slotting them into computer-written envelopes. "Overflow," said Eve blithely.

Hundreds upon hundreds of "Believe in Eve" posters bloomed and sprouted in purple glory in the gardens and windows of the party faithful, competing valiantly with the orange "Forward with Fiona" display of the United Party. And to everyone's alarm the visit of the Chancellor of the Exchequer was confirmed for the Saturday immediately preceding election day. A Campaign Bus was to be provided for the occasion. It was very ominous indeed.

It was just five days before this, at the breakfast table, that Eve announced that she simply *must* get back by nine that evening; there was a United Party Political Broadcast scheduled, about which there had already been much ado. The public had been titillated by tantalizing trailers and sneak previews; it was rumoured to be the greatest Broadcast of all time. "And I can't bear to miss it," said Eve. "I'll have to rush my doorsteps." Doorsteps were the all-important door-to-door interviews.

"Do you have to do every single doorstep in the whole constituency?" asked Tonia, looking up from the Find the M.P. puzzle she was in the process of solving. This had arrived in the morning post. Marcus was similarly occupied in circling twelve differences between two pictures of the Home Secretary kissing an outraged-looking baby.

"Oh, Tonia, of course not, that's what the computer's for. It's programmed to eliminate all the rock-solid Democrats and Uniteds. I only go to houses where there is a possible Floating Voter."

"This entire jamboree," said Tom Archer, "is being run for the benefit of the Floating Voter."

"Yes, precisely," said Eve. "No point bothering with the unpersuadables."

"Voting Floater," said Marcus, thoughtfully, and then: "I'd like to see the computer. What else does it do?"

"It's amazingly clever. We programmed it with masses of information on every single constituent – age, job, children if any, N.H.S. or private, financial status, interests and hobbies – and it produces an individual letter for each of them. Marvellous. I mean, with a young couple we give them all the gumph about mortgage relief, family benefits, education – but it would be a waste of time telling that to a pensioner, wouldn't it? And our policy on unions, say, is put quite differently, depending on whether it's aimed at a union member or a managing director. Ethnic minorities get the full race relations bit."

"Who gets the truth?" asked Russell in his habitual mumble, but nobody noticed. He was eating one of the banana yogurts which had replaced raspberry jelly as a staple of his diet. The yogurt was a sickly yellow with little lumps in it.

"And of course," Eve was saying, "we send out regular Democrat Newsletters to all children over twelve. Very impressionable years, twelve to seventeen. And did you know," she added with pride, "the computer has isolated the two hundred *most* marginal families and invited all their children to a Democrat Children's Party on election eve. Now that *is* smart."

"It's futile," said Russell. "The United Party are sending out a Giant United Bumper Fun Pack to all children aged seven to ten. With inflatable Jim Burton balloons" – Jim Burton was the United leader – "and working toy voting-machines."

"Oh, *Russell*," said his father, "don't be such a wet blanket."

"*And*," said Russell, leaning back and gazing, mournfully, at his yogurt pot, "it's just the same with the Democrat Lucky Bonanza Ballot Lottery. The United Party are doing Election Bingo. It's so totally futile. It all cancels itself out. If the whole lot of you were to sit back and do nothing, it would all work out exactly the same in the end." This seemed like a good exit line, so he got up and left the room, with a dim sense of having exposed some great and hitherto unsuspected truth.

Eve zoomed through her doorsteps in record time, charming a fair number of suspicious Floaters along the way, and arrived home just in time to summon Russell downstairs for the Broadcast. "Russell, darling, this isolation isn't healthy. Even a teenager needs some interaction with the family. No man is an island, Russell!"

"He still hasn't changed those socks!" said Tom Archer, as Russell folded himself furtively into an armchair. Only ten minutes, he thought.

"Hush," said Marcus. "It's starting." They all turned to face the TV. The opening shot was of a Monopoly board. The camera zoomed in to a close-up.

"It's a dicey business, living under Democrat rule," the commentator said menacingly. "Here is the British Voter."

A little man ran on to the starting square. "You have just passed GO. You have collected £200." A giant hand presented the Voter with a wad of notes; he squeaked with delight. "But for how long will you be allowed to keep it?" The Voter set off doggedly on a circuit of the board. The Old Kent Road was occupied by the Minister for Administration and Bureaucracy; he reached out and snatched a few notes from the Voter, whose face fell. In the Whitechapel Road he encountered the Minister for the Aged, who did the same. In the Income Tax square lurked the Chancellor of the Exchequer; the Voter gave a scream of anguish, and raced past at speed, arriving breathless and exhausted at King's Cross Station, where the Minister for Transport was waiting for him. Dejectedly the Voter plodded on with his steadily diminishing load; as he passed through the various Monopoly sites the Ministers for Energy, Social Services, Education and Defence grabbed a handful of his money, and settled down gleefully to count their spoils.

"If anybody but the Government were to try to steal your hard-earned income," the commentator said, "what would happen to them? They would Go to Jail!" The giant hand reappeared, holding, by the scruff of the neck, a wriggling, kicking Chancellor of the Exchequer, and deposited him firmly in Jail. It was a most brilliant use of trick photography. The Chancellor rattled the bars, and sat down miserably to contemplate his crimes. The row of Ministers all looked doleful at the sight of their incarcerated Chancellor; the Voter, left with just one ten pound note, burst into tears.

"*Nobody* wins with the Democrats," the commentator concluded. "Don't play games with your future!" The broadcast ended with an announcement that this Party Political was now available as a record, video-cassette or cartridge, from all good stores.

"Oh, I *liked* that," said Tonia.

"Damn clever," said her father. "Pity it was them, and not us."

"I could weep," said Eve. "It's the worst possible thing. And Angus—poor Angus—coming on Saturday. Here. It's terrible. God knows how many votes he'll lose me."

"Perhaps he'll commit suicide," said Tom. And that was the most cheerful idea anyone could come up with.

Reaction in the country to this broadcast was instantaneous and remarkable. Sales of Monopoly sets tripled, and the makers received many irate letters from purchasers who had expected that their set would contain a Chancellor; it was rumoured that the Chancellor of the Exchequer was a broken man. A record, "I Wanna be Free" by the Chancellors, was rush-released. Little metal puzzles appeared: Get the Chancellor Out. Chancellor overalls, liberally splattered with arrows, were to be seen in the most chic of boutiques. It was truly astonishing.

Russell arrived home on the day before the Chancellor's visit to the unpleasant sight of Sandy Coppard, roaring up and down like a frenzied bull, while his mother made soothing noises from a safe distance. It soon emerged that Sandy, as his agent, had been claiming the Chancellor's right to a royalty on all the Chancellor items, and copyright fees for the use of his name. All her efforts had been in vain; her present suffering was due to the thought of all those piles and piles of cash that she wasn't going to get ten per cent of. And the Chancellor's image, already appalling, had now been damaged beyond repair. It was a bleak time for Sandy.

"And now this!" she shrieked, waving the early edition of the *Chorwell Journal*. "You!" she hissed at Russell. "The black sheep!"

"That's right, blame me," said Russell. Everyone always did.

"'The mystery surrounding Eve Carroll's shady eldest

76

child,'" read Sandy, with venom. "'Why has Russell Archer failed to appear at his mother's side at any time during the campaign? Why is he missing from the campaign photograph? Is there something we should be told?'"

"Well, that's your fault, isn't it?" said Russell. "You were the one that wanted to keep Mum looking youthful, remember?"

"'Why are Russell's family so anxious to hide him away? . . .'"

"Well, that'll teach you to start all this lousy muckraking, then," said Russell, feeling a spark of something he distantly remembered as being called animation. "You and that glue-sniffing stuff. See where it's got you now?"

"Now, Sandy," said Eve, as Sandy began to paw the carpet, apparently in preparation for a charge. "Why don't you pop along down to HQ and check up with John on the timetable for tomorrow, and I'll have a quiet word with Russell." Somehow she steered Sandy to the front door. Poor John, thought Russell, as Sandy stormed off down the path. "Stupid cow," he said, as his mother returned.

"Yes, darling, I know. Well done. Marvellous, to see you showing some spirit. I always knew you had it in you." She hesitated. "But, Russell – I'm really in quite a bit of trouble, here. I mean, I need your help."

"Mine?"

"Russell – we – I want you to come along tomorrow. I want you to ride with me and the Chancellor in the Campaign Bus."

"I'd sooner die," said Russell.

"Oh, *Russell*," said Tonia. She and Marcus had been in the kitchen, listening with great relish. "Come on. It'll be gorgeous fun."

"Eggs," said Russell, meaningfully.

"Actually," said Eve, "I want Russell on his own. Just

77

Russell. Not you two. I think Russell really needs to be *featured*. To shut up those idiotic journalists."

"But we've got..." said Marcus, and stopped abruptly.

"Will you, Russell? It's very important, darling. I promise I shan't ask *any*thing more of you, if you'll do this one thing."

"Eggs," said Russell.

"Yes," said Eve with characteristic honesty, "I expect there will be quite a few eggs flying around, one way and another." Marcus and Tonia exchanged glances of bitter disappointment.

"If I do it," saidRussell, slowly, "you'll leave me alone. You won't make me integrate with the family. You'll leave me to disintegrate upstairs. You'll..."

"Anything! Oh, Russell, I knew you wouldn't let me down!"

"I must be mad," said Russell, and slunk from the room before his mother had a chance to hug him. She was always trying to hug him. It was putrid.

Saturday dawned wet and drizzly and cold. Russell had expected this. It was probably going to be the worst day of his life. He'd slept badly. In his dreams he was attacked by giant eggs, their yolks splattering in a livid sunburst on his face. After breakfast Tonia offered him a carrier bag, which proved to contain three dozen eggs for retaliation purposes, and a large bat, to be used for self-defence. She and Marcus had been looking forward to using these from the top of the bus. Russell refused them. "I'm not into violence," he said, wanly. If, he thought, he was to suffer, then he would be seen to suffer. If he was to be made a fool of in the eyes of the whole town, then let it be as a hapless victim, not one of the warmongers.

The plan was this: the Chancellor and his retinue would be met at a secret rendezvous, and conveyed by car to the bus, a lurid purple open-topped double decker, which was waiting in Southwood Gardens. There would then be a Triumphal Drive along the High Street and right through the town centre, followed by an informal lunch at Eve's house. The Chancellor would then proceed to the Town Hall for a speech and a question-and-answer session. Russell was to be spared this; he would be freed after the Drive.

The Chancellor was waiting patiently at the rendezvous, looking, Russell thought, even smaller and more ineffectual than he did on television, if such was possible. "*Angus*," said Eve, shaking his hand. "*So* pleased you could come – such a terrible week – the Broadcast – jail – simply awful for you – poor Angus – meet my son Russell." Russell and the Chancellor nodded at each other. Russell was wearing a sweat shirt which said: SUPPORT DISABLED GAY ONE-PARENT FAMILY ETHNIC WHALES.

The Chancellor's retinue consisted of a bodyguard, a speech-writer, several secretaries and a party official. Several journalists were also present. It soon became clear that only the bodyguard was travelling on the bus. The others insisted that they would do far better to ride in the cars. The people, they said anxiously, must have an unimpeded view of their Chancellor. As for Sandy, there was no sign of her. She had phoned through that morning with a garbled message about the England cricket captain needing her advice; she would try to join them for lunch.

'Well, here we go," said the Chancellor miserably, as they climbed into the bus, and up the stairs. There were no seats on top. The bus felt very empty, with just the four of them and the driver; Russell felt exposed, up there at the mercy of the elements. What on earth was he doing here? How had she persuaded him? It was all Sandy's fault. He would never forget that. Always assuming that he survived.

The engines revved; slowly the procession moved off.

79

Purple balloons and banners streamed from the railing. Russell was freezing.

"How shall we stand?" asked Eve. "Perhaps if you stay there on the left, Russell, and Angus and myself here on the right..."

"No, no," said the Chancellor gallantly. "Such a nice suit you're wearing, Eve. It might be better if you were to join Russell on the left." Already a roaring noise could be heard in the distance. Eve crossed hastily to Russell's side. "Practise waving, dear," she urged.

Waving? Who in their right mind would want Russell Archer waving at them? Feebly he waggled his right arm up and down, feeling the mocking eyes of the muscle-mountain bodyguard focused on his matchstick biceps. The roaring grew louder.

"Sounds like a mob riot," said the Chancellor, mournfully. "I've never had a riot before." Everyone but the bodyguard began to look nervous. Eve switched on the tape and the "Democrat Marching Tune" began to play through the loudspeakers, but the roaring was reaching an undrownable volume. Russell wondered if it would actually make any difference to anything if he were to fling himself over the rail, here and now. The noise seemed, as they approached the north end of the High Street, to be forming itself into a regular chant.

"What are they saying?" called Eve.

"It's probably 'Kill the Chancellor'," shouted the Chancellor. "That's the usual ... no. It's different. Longer."

"Perhaps it's 'Kill the Chancellor slowly,'" suggested Eve. The Chancellor gripped the rail more tightly. They could see the people now. There must have been thousands; pressed ten deep against the shop fronts, shrieking and waving flags and banners, leaning from first and second floor windows – a terrifying sight.

"I want to go home," whispered Russell. The bodyguard looked scornful. They had almost reached the jeering mob, now. They were...

"Listen," said Eve Carroll, softly. "Angus – Russell – listen to the words." Russell listened. And unbelievably, what he heard was this:

"We love the Chancellor! Free the Chancellor! We love the Chancellor!"

"The natives," said Eve, breaking into an impish grin, "are friendly." And suddenly it was all quite different. The crowds were not jeering, but cheering. They were practically demented. "We love the Chancellor!" rang out on all sides as the bus with its dazed occupants inched along the High Street. The banners bore the same message. Chancellor overalls abounded. One swaying section of the crowd was waving Monopoly boards over their heads, in the manner of football fans waving scarves. Giant keys were brandished. "Free the Chancellor!"

"Angus," said Eve, "you are a star." And the Chancellor – the Chancellor was smiling. As if of their own accord, those long-unused facial muscles raised his lips into a curve. In glorious triumph, he waved to the people of Chorwell. The Chancellor was happy.

Russell's first thought was that this just proved the idiocy of the general public. His second and third thoughts were similar. But nonetheless, he found his arm doing a passable imitation of a wave. For some seconds he didn't even notice his mother's arm around his shoulders. And when he did, he couldn't quite bring himself to do anything about it. The tinkling of the Marching Tune and the ecstatic cries of the crowds merged, wafting him out of his normal character. For at least ten minutes, Russell ceased to be depressed. It was a shattering experience.

When they reached home, all three of them felt totally drained, yet unquenchably euphoric. They thought they had left all the people behind, but as the Chancellor alighted from the platform a young girl rushed up to him, carrying a large cake. The Chancellor stepped back, alarmed. Experience had taught him that the combination of general public and foodstuffs were almost invariably damaging to his dignity. But no; the girl merely pressed the cake into his trembling hands, whispered: "I've hidden a file in it" and, leaning forward, kissed him roundly on the cheek. "Hotlips!" she cried, as the Press cameras flashed maniacally.

"Hotlips?" repeated the Chancellor, bewildered. And then: "Eve, I am loved."

"Come inside," hissed Eve, propelling him towards the front door. The retinue had been delayed by the crowds, and were still some minutes away. The Chancellor moved forward as if in a dream. "I am loved," he repeated at intervals.

"But how amazing," said Eve in wonder, as she slammed the front door. "And that must all be as a result of the Broadcast – the United Party have made you a cult figure, Angus! There'll be mayhem in the Shadow Cabinet, when they realize."

"I am loved," said the Chancellor, obstinately. Eve scratched her head. The house, she realized, was empty. Tom and the children had gone to local HQ, where Marcus and Tonia were being shown the computer. They must have been held up by the crowds, too. And Eve needed desperately to use the lavatory. She made a momentous decision.

"Russell," she said, pointing him towards the garden room. "Entertain the Chancellor."

The Chancellor sat on one end of the settee. Russell sat on the other. They looked at each other. "D'you want a Moon of Saturn?" asked Russell.

"Shall I be a devil?" The Chancellor took a Phoebe, and

unwrapped it with interest. "Delicious," he said, munching like a starved man. "Spoil my lunch. Can I have another?"

"You're a right little raver when you get going, aren't you?" Russell tossed over a Rhea.

"Hotlips," said the Chancellor, wistfully.

"Quite a day," said Russell.

"Extraordinary. All these years – eggs – abuse – loathing – and now this."

"You enjoy all that politics lark, do you?"

"Not much," said the Chancellor. "Many's the time I've almost given it up. It all seems – so totally futile, sometimes."

Russell blinked. "But that's my word!"

"It's a good one, isn't it? But one has, in the end, to do something. And," he added, poker-faced, "it certainly beats working for a living."

"Everything's futile, when you really think about it," said Russell.

"My own philosophy exactly." The Chancellor nodded. "You know – you remind me very strongly of myself, at your age."

"Did you change your socks?" asked Russell.

"Never," said the Chancellor. "I couldn't seem to find the energy. What a splendid boy you are. Eve must be so proud of you. And indeed," he added hastily, "you of her. A wonderful woman. A tragedy if she loses her seat. I understand that in that unhappy event she plans to accept the chairpersonship of the Pornography Reform League. Their gain would be our loss."

"She *what*?" said Russell, but at that moment the door banged and people began to pour in: the retinue, closely followed by Sandy Coppard.

"Oh, Chancellor!" In rushed a secretary. "You – you won't need to change your suit, then."

"Clearly not," said the Chancellor, a trifle smugly. "All

those spare clothes you've brought along to no avail, Vernon. As they say, the yolk's on you."

The party gaped. Spontaneous wit? From their *Chancellor*? "Yes, Maureen? What's the trouble?"

The speech-writer stepped forward. "Your speech, Chancellor – it'll have to be changed – it won't do at all!"

"Why?" asked the Chancellor, taking the paper. "'I would like,'" he read, "'to thank the people of Chorwell for your marvellous welcome. I have always been most partial to omelettes...'"

"I'll rewrite the whole thing," said Maureen, and darted from the room.

"Well, Sandy," said the Chancellor. "You see, you could very well have come along after all."

"Cricket captain," said Sandy, looking uncomfortable. "Urgent – sponsorship – winter tour of Australia – new hairstyle..."

"Stumped, aren't you, Sandy? One silly point after another!" The secretaries hastily jotted down "stumped – silly point". It might come in useful.

"But it was the most tremendous success!" said Sandy, unabashed.

"No thanks to you," said the Chancellor. "And there is Eve, calling us to lunch. Being a star works up the appetite, Sandy. Come, Russell. I insist that you sit at my right hand. Marvellous youngster," he said.

"You're joking," said Sandy.

"I can't seem to stop, can I? Come, Russell. I am loved."

"And so the swing to the United Party in Wigan 8.9, *very* close to our computer prediction..."

Russell, sprawled awkwardly on his bed, stared at the IMP's screen in total misery. It was as bad as it could possibly be. Result after result was confirming the trend; the country was at the dawn of a new period of United rule.

84

Democrat marginals were falling like ninepins. The Chorwell result, due in about five minutes, was, now, a foregone conclusion. Eve Carroll was doomed.

He was quite alone. His father was at the Town Hall with his mother; Marcus and Tonia in bed asleep. They had school tomorrow. So did Russell, come to that – foul, obnoxious thought. He would have to leave, he decided. He'd do the exams, and then slink off and never be seen again. He couldn't cope with the Pornography Reform League.

Nobody understood; nobody cared. He'd tried to explain to the IMP, but the word "pornography" wasn't in its vocabulary. He could have explained by means of the Concept System, but he was too embarrassed. He didn't really have that sort of relationship with the IMP – and it would undoubtedly flash its little green lights in a sniggery nudge-nudge sort of way – no.

"Another voting machine broken down in Ealing," said the programme presenter – "a manual count now going on in Ealing. Now I understand we're ready to join Jill McEwan in Chorwell where they're ready for a declaration . . ."

Russell gave a little moan of distress. He barely heard the opening words of the returning officer, nor his mother's vote total, nor those of her opponents. He just saw her face, resilient, determined, cheerful in the very jaws of defeat, up there on the platform behind her purple rosette. Only when the words "DEM HOLD CHORWELL" flashed gigantic across the screen did it register. Blearily, bewildered, he sat up. His mother was walking to the microphone, glowing with exuberant triumph. She began to thank people. The workers, agents, the party faithful. "And my wonderful family – my husband Tom, my children, Tonia and Marcus." Oh. Fine. Fine, thought Russell, who had never yet had a jug of iced water emptied down the back of his

85

neck, but now knew what it would feel like. Charming, thought Russell, and sniffed.

"And finally," said Eve, "a word about two very special people, who shared with me in that momentous event which I believe was a major cause of the Democrats regaining Chorwell against every indication from early results all over the country. Firstly, my dear friend Angus Craig, the Chancellor of the..." There was a delighted cry of "Free the Chancellor!" from the Democrats in the hall. Eve smiled. "Yes. A wonderful man. And secondly, my son Russell, who showed at a critical moment just how richly blessed he is with character, loyalty and courage, surprising many people, including, I think, himself. Our victory is his victory. Thank you, Russell."

Russell flung himself at the IMP and switched off. Stupid nurd! Blah blah blah with half the nation listening – the shame! – and it hadn't been him anyway, it was the Chancellor's personal presence and that alone which had caused this incredible upset of a result ... confused, he scrambled into bed and buried his head under the blankets. No Reform League, he thought. Five years in Opposition probably. No Junior Ministry. No more blame. It was – well, not too bad. If only she hadn't gone and said all that lot of dreadful things ... and yet, the words "character", "loyalty" and "courage" kept returning to him, no matter how he fought to shut them out. Finally he gave in and sat up. The evening was incomplete. It needed some small gesture on his part, a silent acknowledgement of – of something. Russell made the gesture. He changed his socks.

REPUTATION

There's always a special atmosphere in the classroom just before the very last of the summer exams. There's the united, comradely feeling that comes from enduring the most terrible torment together, mixed with the fact that it's so very nearly over. You feel almost jovial as you turn over the paper and scan the last set of questions; now you know the worst, and the exams have lost one of their deadliest weapons, the capacity to surprise you. Add to this the knowledge that those awful panicky evenings of desperation, dread and endless revision are finally behind you – tonight you will be free. Ahead lies a beautiful, unshadowed weekend – the summer holidays are only a few weeks away, and no more exams for what seems like an eternity. No wonder that the teachers look especially stern, and bark: "You haven't finished your exams yet, you know!" It makes no difference.

But it wasn't quite like that for me in the Third Year, because that last exam was by far the most important. It was on Friday morning, and it was German. As we dumped our bags at the front of the classroom, and arranged ourselves skilfully into alphabetical order at the desks, clutching pencil cases and rulers and blotting paper, I discovered that I felt worse than I had all week. As I settled down into the desk behind Claire Robson, and tried to feel at home, I could see that my hands were actually shaking. It was that bad. My attempt at writing my name and form in the top right-hand corner of a piece of exam paper looked like the work of a team of inebriated spiders. Because this one was different – this was German, and great things were expected. Of me.

We'd only started doing German that year, which was going to make it a lot more difficult at O Level than French, which we'd done right from the start. For this reason, only selected people would be given the option of carrying on with it in the fourth; the selection would, of course, be largely based on this exam result. Because of timetable complications, doing German O Level meant dropping History. This prospect was a great joy to me, because as far as I was concerned History was *the* most uninteresting subject, saving only French, which drove me half out of my tiny mind with boredom. So obviously it was important to get a good mark.

But that wasn't exactly the problem. If I was lucid and logical about it – though this was difficult – I knew I really couldn't help but do well. I seemed to have a natural gift for German. Right from the start I'd taken to it. I'd grasped the rules of grammar with astounding ease – it astounded me anyway – and the vocabulary seemed to learn itself. I came top in every single test, all year. It was a new and marvellous experience. It's not that I'm particularly thick, just that there are always other people better than me, at everything. Not necessarily the same people, but always somebody. I usually came somewhere between sixth and twelfth. Very respectable. But inside I always wanted to be the best. At *anything*.

So it was very, very lucky that I was put into the German set, especially since my French was so dismal. I wasn't expecting anything of German. I'd assumed that being bad at French meant being bad at all languages. Dangerous things, generalizations. And I loved it all. I loved the fact that Mrs. Sparkes was obviously delighted to have discovered me, just as the Science staff were with Maria Corbin. And I'd always remembered that gleam that came into Thunderthighs Townsend's – our games mistress's – eye the first time she saw Hannah Broome wield a hockey stick. I wanted that gleam. I *pined* to be discovered. And now I had been, and I was rapidly learning the great disadvantage. The pressure. I was *expected* to do superbly well at this exam. I was expected to be top. I had my reputation to consider now – the only reputation I'd ever had since the first year, when I accidentally set fire to Laura Newbolt in Chemistry, and acquired a temporary reputation as an arsonist, tending towards the homicidal. This was glory. It was *well* worth the fearful row, and being forbidden to touch a Bunsen burner for the rest of the term. It was, until German, my finest hour. (Laura was only singed, and survived to continue waving her fat little arm about and saying "Please, Miss, please, Miss.") So it was absolutely imperative that I do well in this exam. No wonder my nerves were twanging, and my guts doing an intestinal interpretation of the can-can. I felt like *death*.

We had some dumpy elderly dame from Science Block called Mrs. Price sitting with us. She looked bored and grim and very very nasty. Round the room she plodded, slapping a question paper face down on each desk – "and don't turn them over!" she snapped, as if we didn't know. "And make sure you've plenty of writing paper. I shall be very annoyed if I have to jump up and down giving people more." Back to the front she stumped, and looked at the clock. "Nine twenty-six. I think we'll wait till half past." Grimaces flashed surreptitiously around the room. Everyone wanted to get on with it, not sit there for another four minutes, sweating. Ponderously the dame heaved her mighty bulk to the blackboard and wrote: "Form K3. German." (We knew this.) "Began 9.30. Ends 11.15." We sat, as if mesmerized, watching. The clock ticked round. Half past. "You may begin."

There was a rustling, followed by a morbid silence. I reached for the paper, two duplicated sheets stapled together, turned it, and read 'German. Third Year' – and then the first question. And suddenly it was all right. My head stopped swimming, my hands steadied. This was all right. I could do this.

And I enjoyed it. I really did. There's something deeply satisfying about dealing with an exam paper with competence and confidence. You feel in control of it. Of course I knew I'd made mistakes. There were a couple of strange words that were difficult to deduce from the context, and some plurals I couldn't remember. All these I guessed. There was also a short piece of German prose for comprehension, followed by questions to be answered in German *without* copying word for word from the passage. It's just about impossible to do this without mistakes. But I felt I'd had a pretty good go at it. Triumphantly, I wrote the very last answer. It was over, and it couldn't really have gone much better. All that worrying. All for nothing. Now, just go through once more checking, and ... I glanced at the clock, for the first time. I'd been too absorbed before. Twenty past ten, it said. *Twenty past ten.* I'd finished the damn thing in fifty minutes.

I didn't like this. It was less than half the allotted time – surely that wasn't possible? Could my question paper have a sheet missing? No, there were obviously only two, the second one was only two-thirds covered. I looked around. Everyone else was either writing or sort of quietly tearing their hair. So it was just me. Oh. Well. I was supposed to be the best, but this was ridiculous. The only thing to do was to go through the whole thing again, slowly, carefully. I must have been working *much* too fast.

So I covered my answers, and redid the paper, working each question out in my head before checking it with what I'd written. I double checked every word-ending. All I found was three mistakes. No more than that. And I don't know if I'd expected this process to take another fifty minutes, but it doesn't work like that, not when you've just done it all once, and when I'd finished it was still only twenty-five to eleven. Forty minutes left. Forty minutes of sitting still, doing absolutely nothing. Awful. I could never understand why they wouldn't let people go out when they'd finished. Such a pointless waste of time. Probably they thought people would give up more easily, or just rush it so as to get away. But these didn't seem very powerful arguments to me, stuck there, marooned on an island desk with nothing to do but watch the creeping clock.

I sat back, keeping hold of my pen so as not to look too conspicuous. Various vague thoughts drifted through my mind. The oddness of an exam lasting one and three-quarter hours; all the rest had been multiples of half an hour. I was pleased with German for being different. The chilling, menacing appearance of the desks in their exam formation, as far apart as possible, so different from their usual friendly pairs. I was in the back row, where I could see almost everything. In front of me Claire Robson's pony-tail hung down like a moth-eaten bellpull. My immediate neighbours to the left and right were Laura Newbolt and Justine Webb. I slid my eyes left, without moving my head. Laura was frowning and pouting and pursing and sucking her lips, a medley of her 'ooh but I'm really *trying*' expressions playing over her snouty little features. She still hadn't turned to the second page of questions. She tapped her teeth with her pen top and pulled at her right ear. This seemed to bring no inspiration, so she stuck her tongue out, reached for her hair, which was long and snarled with tangles, selected a lock with care and began to chew it with determination. I couldn't quite bear this, so I looked away and glanced to my right, to Justine Webb.

The truth that people grow up at very different speeds could not be more clearly illustrated than by Justine and me being in the same class. It made a joke out of chronological age. Actually, I was four months older. But when we were both put into K3 there might have been a decade between us. I'm going to have to be brutally honest here. They do say it's good for the character. At thirteen I was a total infant. I'd cleverly stopped wearing white socks, but just the same I rushed home to see Blue Peter, and got all worked up about opening my stocking at Christmas time. Probably being the youngest of five children had a lot to do with it. My favourite book was still, firmly, *Ballet Shoes*. Show me a beach and – yes – I'd build a sandcastle. I couldn't quite fill a size 32A bra. That was me.

Justine was like an adult. Her very presence at school always seemed highly incongruous. She had a deep, husky voice, knowing eyes ringed with heavy dark circles, and a weary face. Whereas I hadn't yet become interested in boys, Justine had already graduated to men. I saw her out with one once, in the Broadway. She was wearing a long skirt and a low-cut blouse, and looking about twenty. I was rather touched that she smiled at me, kindly, as I passed. Several people told me that she'd already had an abortion. I'd also heard that she'd attempted suicide twice. I knew for a fact that every Tuesday afternoon, while the rest of us did Games, Justine went off to her psychiatrist in Harley Street to be analysed. This seemed to me to be the very height of sophistication.

I wasn't envious of her – she was simply too far removed from me. She sat at the back of the classroom, I sat at the front; we moved around the school in the same groups, but our paths seldom crossed. Third Years are very clannish. Nor did I exactly admire her, but she had a great deal of status, did Justine. I suppose my attitude could best be described as a sort of uncomprehending respect, distant, and tinged with occasional curiosity.

Justine was also a genius. This subtly added to her prestige. She was a twofold genius, at Art and English. Her drawings and paintings were exquisite, wild, brilliant. Her people not only looked like people, they had real expressions. Justine could draw anger and pain and love. It was rather wonderful. Most of her pictures, though, tended towards the mystical and the abstract. This was also the case with her compositions in English. I wasn't so enthusiastic about Justine's writing, largely because I never understood a word of it. Mrs. Raymond, however, would praise to high heaven Justine's use of allegory and powerful imagery, and I never doubted that her work was marvellous, because I'd learned that whenever I found a book incomprehensible it was almost certainly very highly thought of, and probably a classic.

So here, too, I accepted that Justine moved in a different sphere from myself. I think that her being a genius made the authorities slightly more tolerant of her than they would otherwise have been. After all, she'd been in some trouble, one way and another. For instance, in the second year she was caught cheating in the Maths exam, and nothing so very terrible happened to her. She was a total idiot at Maths and Science, but perhaps they thought that with her other talents, it wasn't really important.

Anyhow, Justine clearly had that elusive thing, a reputation. As I swivelled my eyeballs sharp right I wouldn't exactly have been *surprised* to see her surreptitiously jabbing a hypodermic into a vein – everyone knew Justine was on drugs. But she was just sitting there, her uniform looking as always like a humorous accident, her hair a fair frothy frizzy cloud, her face forlorn as she scribbled on her blotting paper. I wondered why. We were allowed to use all the rough paper we wanted. Whatever she was up to, she was writing very purposefully. As if sensing my curiosity, she shifted the blotting paper over to the very edge of the desk, nearer to me. I could read it now. She'd written: "Is Hand der die or das?"

I whipped my eyes back to my own desk and studied my paper intently. I could feel a trace of flush creeping over my face. Justine – Justine Webb was asking for my help. It was rather flattering that she should need my help in anything. But it wasn't helping, was it? Cheating was what it was, and disqualification, hell fire and disgrace if I got caught. I didn't want anything to do with that. I couldn't risk it. The ethical side of it didn't cross my mind. Ethics weren't my strong point. I was just terrified of getting caught.

And yet there was Justine, waiting. What could I do? For all I knew Justine and her mates carried on like this the whole time. And I wanted very badly to be known as the sort of person who's not afraid to – help someone out. A reputation as a goody-goody priggish little Miss Righteous was the *last* thing I needed. My identity was slight enough without that. My character would be annihilated. I'd have to do it.

It would surely be all right. We were miles away from the Price woman, lugubriously marking her paper up at the front. But all the same, the moment I uncapped my pen and reached for the blotting paper I felt a hundred eyes boring through the wall behind me, most of them belonging to our Headmistress Miss Browne, the Education Authority's equivalent of Argus. A semi-circle of huge red arrows appeared in formation over my head. I blinked and wrote "Die", which just about summed up my feelings. I didn't look at her. I wrote good and big so she couldn't miss it, left it in open view for ten seconds, and then set to work obliterating it with a felt tip, thinking that was *that*, and at least I knew I'd given her the right answer.

What Justine had been asking was the gender of the German word *Hand*, which means – shock and amazement – "hand". German nouns can be masculine, feminine or neuter – *die* means "the" with a feminine noun – and it's all crazily illogical. An apple is a he, an orange a she, a girl an it. I worked out a terrific system for remembering this. If a word is masculine I made a picture of it with a male person, if feminine a female person, if neuter an animal. For example, a car is neuter, so my car picture was an elephant in a Mini. If it had been feminine I'd have had something like Thunderthighs doing press-ups on the roof of a Volkswagen. The dafter the picture the better, and it really worked. My 'hand' picture was a giant hand reaching down from the sky and throttling Laura Newbolt.

It was still only ten to eleven. I wished desperately for the exam to be finished. I wanted to get out of that room, remove myself from the scene of the crime. I was very uneasy about being next to Justine. I glanced quickly in her direction, and immediately wished I hadn't. For the blotting paper was back in position, and written on it: "What does *Kreis* mean?"

This wasn't fair. Once, yes. Twice was taking advantage. Why should I put myself at risk for *her* – and yet, the old arguments still stood. It was the sheer strength of Justine's prestige that made me so helpless. I drew an angry little circle on the blotting paper. If she didn't get the message, that was tough.

If I'd used my sense, I shouldn't have looked up from that point until the papers were collected. But I was in no condition to be sensible, by then. My nerve had gone; I was restless and unhappy and very uneasy. I continued to dart little jittery glances over to my right. I wanted to be absolutely sure that Justine had covered up the evidence as thoroughly as I had. Surely she couldn't be so dumb as to leave it there on the blotting paper? I couldn't *see* the blotting paper. What had she...

Mrs. Price cleared her throat. My eyes jerked to the front. She was staring directly at me. My stomach gave a little shudder. I was stiff with fright. Her cold, cold eyes were pinioning me across the length of the classroom, alert, unblinking and full of dislike. I didn't know what to do, think, anything. I dropped my head, trying to behave innocently – casually – and began to doodle on the blotting paper. This seemed best – she may have seen – the blotting paper – best to be using it for doodling, I'd been doodling all along...

Mrs. Price rose heavily to her feet. My insides gave another squelch; my hand seemed to be operating independently of the rest of me. I had nothing to do with it. She was *coming*. But in a moment I realized that she had in fact gone to the other side of the room. I dared a quick glance, and saw that she was giving out the string, string to tie our answer papers together. It seemed commonplace enough, and yet I knew she would not pass me by. Not after that look she'd given me. Up and down the rows she waddled, round the corner, up our aisle, past Claire, string on Claire's desk ... she stopped, took my answer sheets and pulled them roughly round until they faced her. Her horrid tight face – her cheeks covered with brown marks, like freckles that had decided to launch an offensive and bid for more territory – came closer as she peered at it, then turned it back, dropped a piece of string in contemptuous fashion, and moved on.

I knew what that was all about – she wanted to find out my name. It was serious, then. And yet for a few mad moments my only feeling was one of outrage, of hate for that old hag for mauling my beautiful German paper with her filthy hand. I noticed that she didn't pause at Justine's desk, and the fury soon gave way to fear and dread as I realized that Justine had landed *me* in it, while she, the *experienced* cheat, had been skilful enough to get away with it – oh, and it was *German*. My world began, slowly, to fall to pieces around me, as I sat there fighting a desperate battle with the baby tears that were burning and prickling at the back of my eyes and nose. I began to feel very sorry for myself. Fervently I wished that one of Justine's suicide attempts had been successful.

I don't really know how I got through the last quarter of an hour. The worst of it was not knowing what she would do, what would happen, how bad it really was. I couldn't work out what I should say because I didn't know how much, or exactly what she had seen. I thought about some of Miss Browne's choicer remarks on the subject of dishonesty. I thought about what my Mum would say. And nagging away at the back of my mind – the German exam. Apart from the disgrace of disqualification – would I be allowed to do it next year? Surely they couldn't – my only glory. My one reputation. It was a very, very bad time.

"Stop writing," grunted the Price woman. There was a lot of sighing and stretching. "No talking!" The papers were collected. "Pass your blotting paper forward. Now, you may go outside for fifteen minutes' break. Everyone is to be back here by eleven thirty-five. And be quiet! Remember that other people are still working. Not a word until you've left the building."

Uncertainly I rose, slid out of the desk and walked down the aisle. I didn't want to seem to be hurrying, but I didn't half want to get out. Was I to be allowed to go, then? *Act normally.* I reached the front.

"Sayer! Stop where you are, please." I froze. My knees went to a watery jelly. Nobody had ever called me by my surname before. Look innocent, I told myself furiously. Hold your head up. Stand straight.

I got some curious looks as the others filed out. Of course, none of them had the least idea that anything had been happening. "All right," said Mrs. Price as the door was closed. "You were staring at another girl's work. You were constantly looking over, trying to see what she was writing. Don't bother to say anything. You'll be wasting your breath. You've been told often enough what happens in these cases. You're coming along with me now to Miss Browne."

Dumbly I followed her down the corridor and into the hall, across the hall to the offices. "Wait there," she snapped, "and don't speak to anybody." I felt like a contaminant. Various people wandered through the hall, taking no notice of me, carrying on with their carefree lives. I tried to rehearse what I would say to Miss Browne, but my mind wasn't working; all it would say was: "I wasn't copying. I *wasn't*. It's not fair. I wasn't copying. It's not ..."

Back came Price. She seemed to have been gone hours, but my ability to judge time had gone haywire. "Miss Browne will see you at twelve o'clock." I wasn't sure if I was to wait, or to go and come back. I turned, hesitated, stopped. "Well, off you go!" – as if talking to an imbecile. I went. I went outside and breathed in the fresh air. I looked around for my friends; it took me some minutes to realize that their break must be long over, and everyone was back in the classroom.

If I'd expected a funereal silence, I was wrong. They hadn't even bothered to make a collection for my wreath. I found K3 unsupervised and celebrating. The exams were over, and it was Karen Lander's birthday, and she'd brought along a great big box of chocolate almonds, and they were all sitting in the usual little groups, bunched and huddled, on desks and on chairs, stuffing themselves silly and generally having a whale of a time. My best friend

Rosie did have the grace to look concerned. "Where've *you* been?" But before I could tell her I saw Justine, at the back of the room with her mates Big Alice, Shona, Melissa and Desperate Debby, beckoning frantically. So that was where I went.

"What happened? You didn't tell Browne, did you?" She took my arm and drew me confidingly into the circle. Her eyes pierced searchingly into mine. Her lashes were all spiky and sticky with mascara.

"I haven't seen her. I've to go back at twelve." She still had hold of my wrist. It was very subtle psychology. Desperate Debby was only inches away.

"Look, don't say anything. They can't prove a thing, right? They'll never think that you were copying anyway. It's not as if it was me."

"It was you," I said, marvelling at my audacity. Justine's jaw dropped slightly. She got up and walked off to the front of the room, leading me behind her like a well-trained pup. "Listen," she said urgently, putting her arm round my shoulder and drawing me closer. "You really won't tell, will you, because my Dad'll *kill* me. I got into trouble last year, you know, and if it happens again . . ."

And, amazingly, I realized that behind all this clever manoeuvring, this softening-up, the girl was really frightened. She'd gone deathly white, and the two dark rings under her eyes stood out like bruises. It was astonishing. I'd never imagined Justine *having* a Dad, let alone a violent one. I knew nothing about her home and family at all. I'd pictured her doing what she liked, when she liked. And yet it seemed that perhaps she wasn't so very different from the rest of us after all.

"I won't tell," I said. I was feeling more confident by the minute. They *couldn't* prove anything. I *hadn't* been copying. It was only suspicion. You're innocent until proven guilty.

"Oh, thank you! You're great. I knew you were a good

kid." For an awful moment I thought she was going to kiss me. I scuttled over to Rosie, who had, needless to say, been watching all this with bulging eyes and open mouth.

"What's going on? What's all that with Justine?" I told them. "Oh *Gawd*," said Rosie helpfully. "You great nurdle. Here, I saved you a chocolate."

"You didn't really fall for that, did you?" said Claire Robson. "She tried that on me, in Biology."

"Didn't you help her?"

"You're joking. D'you think she'd risk her neck for me? Or for you? I pretended not to see."

"Oh," I said, miserably. It seemed that my calculations had been all wrong. Claire hadn't helped, and *her* reputation hadn't been annihilated. Nobody even *knew* about it, apparently. Oh, I'd made a proper fool of myself.

"You'd better get along to Browne," said Maria Corbin. "It's nearly twelve, look."

"Oh – good luck, then," said Rosie. "It'll be all right," she added, unconvincingly. I could see they were all bursting to have a good gossip as soon as I'd gone. "Honest, would you believe she'd be so daft?" ... "what d'you think'll happen to her?" ... "she's going to be in *awful* trouble" ... all looking suitably shocked and concerned, but inside just dancing with glee, because it wasn't them.

Miss Browne wore large owlish spectacles and had arranged her office in such a way that whoever she was talking to sat fully illuminated, facing the window, while the only light that fell on to her own face slanted obliquely over those lenses, making it impossible to see what her eyes were doing. It put you at a terrible disadvantage. "Sit down," she said, without looking up, as I slid through the door. This was hopeful; sometimes she left people to stand. "Now, I understand from Mrs. Price that you were looking at another girl's work during your German exam this

100

morning. She saw this several times. What have you got to say for yourself?"

"I wasn't copying," I said, automatically.

"Oh, come on, you'll have to do better than that." The opaque lenses flashed. Miss Browne was young, unpredictable and dangerous.

"I know I was looking round. But it wasn't copying. I'd *finished*." Suddenly I realized what my story must be. "I finished at twenty past ten! And it was such a long time until the exam ended – I know I shouldn't have but I wasn't thinking, I just – I got so bored with the view after a while – I couldn't help just looking round a bit just for a change. That's all it was. I didn't think – it was the last exam, you know, and it felt like they were all over." She said nothing, and I couldn't see her eyes. "I'm sorry. I'll never let it happen again."

"Why did you finish so quickly?"

"I don't know – I was surprised, really, that it was so early. I just worked straight through it."

"Hm." She had been fingering a pencil; now she put this down, and clasped her hands. "Well. I've been talking with Mrs. Sparkes. She tells me that in her opinion you're the very last person who would need to cheat. She was very shocked." She paused. "I've seen your marks for the year, and it does seem that the evidence is rather strongly in your favour. In fact, it did cross our minds that a more likely occurrence would be someone else, trying to copy *your* answers. Is that what happened? Did you suspect that Justine Webb was looking at your work?"

"No," I said, truthfully. So she *did* know who the 'other girl' was. "There's absolutely no way she could have done that, Miss Browne. I've got ever so small writing anyway, and my paper would have been hidden by my right arm, the way I was sitting."

"Hm," she said again – not, I thought, completely

101

convinced. Much later, I realized that I had probably protested far too much. "Well. It's very fortunate for you, isn't it, that the subject concerned is the one at which you could be said to be above suspicion. Mrs. Sparkes tells me you're a fast and accurate worker. Your story does have the ring of truth about it. I'll explain the circumstances to Mrs. Price. But remember. If this ever happens again, it'll be a mighty different story. So in future you'd better be jolly careful to keep your eyes to yourself. Understood?"

"Yes." I whispered.

"Very well, then. Oh – before you go. Mrs. Sparkes was really upset to hear that you might have put your exam chances at risk. She feels you're one of the most promising pupils she's ever had. So for goodness sake be especially careful with your best subject in future! You've done remarkably well at German so far. Well done. Now, mind you keep it up."

I almost wished she hadn't tagged that nice bit on to the end. As I left the room I felt really mean. Everything was all right after all, and I should have been bounding with joy, but it wasn't, somehow, like that. I *hadn't* copied – I'd been innocent of the crime, and I'd been cleared of the crime, and yet I felt like a rat and a louse and a skunk. Perhaps this was the first time that I realized that between innocence and guilt there lie many subtle shades of grey.

There are some loose ends to be tied. If I'd expected Justine's undying gratitude I had another think coming. She'd probably forgotten the whole thing by the next day. Nobody seemed to think any more of me for my selfless daring. Those who thought anything at all, thought me foolish. That was my impression.

Justine herself was to follow a course much different from that which I'd imagined for her – something like dropping out of school at the earliest opportunity and ending up half dead in the loos at Piccadilly Circus Underground Station.

In fact, she got eight O Levels and went on to be made a senior prefect, so I suppose all that about the abortion and the drugs and suicide attempts wasn't really true at all, though it was true that she was seeing a psychiatrist. I'm sure I don't know how these things get around. Incidentally, I later found out that her father died when she was seven. She really took me in there. The last I heard of her, she was reading English at Oxford.

And my German exam result? Eighty-four per cent. The person who came second got sixty-nine. So I suppose you could say I saved my reputation after all.

CLEO THE VIGILANT

"And so in the end I spent the night in the bath," said Katie, "and I never did find my socks."

Gina chuckled, sticking her finger in and out of the wire netting that was such an intrinsic part of the décor of the Girls' Cloakroom. It took very little imagination to feel that you were actually in the monkey house at the Zoo: the passage down the side (for visitors); the netting dividing the room into rectangular compartments. Far right: First Years (gibbon) followed by Seconds (Barbary ape), Thirds (marmoset), Fourths... "Katie – someone coming!" hissed Gina in sudden panic. They froze, looking wildly around for some means of escape. There were no means of escape. Not even a coat to hide behind – the coats were all outside on their shivering owners. Which was where Katie and Gina were supposed to be. And in they came, before Katie had time to throw herself to the floor and pretend to be having a fit. In came the prefects.

They entered in formation: in a perfect V like the Red Arrows. And in leading position, at the apex of the V, Cleo Langham. It couldn't have been worse.

"Right! What do you think you're doing indoors? I'm *sick* and *tired* of this insolence from the lower school. You know *perfectly well* you aren't allowed in until the bell." Little angry red dots appeared on Cleo Langham's Persil Automatic whiter-than-white cheeks. The dots looked clownish. "Blatant! Caught red-handed!" You'd think they'd been vandalizing the school building at the very least. "Now out. And consider yourselves lucky I'm not giving you an order mark. But if I *ever* catch you two in here again..." She folded her arms. The two behind promptly folded theirs, too, mixed expressions of dislike and enjoyment flickering over their anonymous, pinched, nonentity prefect faces. Whatever people had looked like in the fifth years, promotion and the prefect tie seemed to do that to them. Their faces changed subtly to fit the mould. Not so Cleo Langham. Her appearance totally belied her nature. Long blonde hair, perfect cameo features in a delicate round face, ivory skin. Only in the pale blue icy eyes was there a clue. Those eyes looked as though they fired lasers. But otherwise – the face of an angel, and the nature of a particularly tyrannical dictator. There was a joke in the third year that Cleo Langham was campaigning for prefects to be armed with sub-machine guns, and given permission to shoot on sight. She'd enjoy that, would Cleo.

"Move!"

They got to their feet. It would certainly have been wisest to exit, shamefaced and speechless, with all possible speed. But this was not in Katie's nature. "It's terribly cold out, you know," she said. "Said on the radio it might snow, later."

"Tough," said Cleo. The flunkeys nodded; well said, Cleo. "Won't do you any harm. Nobody ever died of the cold."

This was so plainly ridiculous that Katie couldn't help laughing, although she knew full well what a perilous thing this was to do. "Scott of the Antarctic," she said. "Captain Oates," she added hopefully.

105

"Don't be cheeky!" One mustn't contradict. If Cleo says that the world is square, start looking for the corners. "Now get out!"

"C'mon," muttered Gina, sensing that Katie was in one of her whimsical, hell-to-the-consequences moods. These were most dangerous. And she was right; as they reached the cloakroom door, their every movement closely watched as if they might produce hand grenades from their coat pockets, Katie hesitated, then turned as if propelled by some force she was powerless to resist, looked Cleo Langham straight in the eye and said, conversationally:

"I think that I shall never see, a prefect uglier than thee."

There was an ominous silence – Gina battling to suppress an explosion of laughter, Katie's eyes sparkling with dread and delight, Cleo standing there in stunned disbelief, while the flunkeys gaped, and exchanged expectant glances.

"Right!" hissed Cleo, finally. "Detention! Gross disrespect! And you..." she glared at Gina ... "can have an order mark." This seemed rather hard, but one does not expect justice from Cleo Langham. Out came the little notebook. "Name and form?"

"Sharon Vaughan, 3H," said Katie.

"Oh, *you're* Sharon Vaughan, are you? I've heard of you. And you?"

"Lucy Connell," said Katie for Gina, who seemed lost for words. Cleo, apparently, considered this quite natural. People *should* be speechless with awe, in the terrible presence of Cleo Langham. "Now get *out*."

Out they went. It *was* cold – bitter, biting cold and still ten minutes before the bell. They set off to walk round the Science Block. If you stood still on a morning like this you'd probably freeze fast to the ground and they'd have to come and hack you away, and take you indoors to melt.

"And what's Sharon Vaughan going to say, when she finds out about that?" Gina banged her gloved hands together, and watched as her breath steamed off into a little cloud.

"She gets so many detentions, she won't even notice one more," said Katie. "And even if she did, she'd be pleased. She'd thank me. She's trying to get herself expelled, didn't you know that?"

"No." Gina didn't really know Sharon Vaughan at all; she was a dark, hefty girl, in a different form from herself and Katie. Katie, however, knew her well; they lived in the same road.

"She can't stand it here. She plays truant half the time. She reckons if they kick her out she'll be able to go to Kendall Lane. She wanted to go there all along. So did I."

"So did I," said Gina, stamping on a tiny frozen puddle. The ice shattered with a crunch; water oozed out murkily. "Nobody at junior school wanted to come to Compton Park. It was the parents."

"Oh, parents think it's fantastic," said Katie crossly, "this stupid uniform, and lots of discipline and *prefects*. *They* haven't got to come here, have they? We do. And naturally nobody asks us. What we think isn't *relevant. Bloody* Cleo Langham," she added, kicking the ground in sudden temper. "Going on about cheek and that. Gross disrespect. She's only three years older than me! Why should I have any respect for her, her with the manners of a pig?"

"Don't be insulting to pigs," said Gina. "Pigs are nice." Gina was always a stout defender of the pig. She believed it to be a much maligned animal, and refused to eat it in any form.

"Quite right," said Katie. "Gross disrespect," she muttered again. "There's only one of me. It takes a hundred and forty-four people, gross disrespect does."

"You'll end up doing Maths O Level yet," said Gina. "No, really though, the way they go on as if they've actually done something, been chosen for some great honour. All you've got to do is survive to the Sixth form to be a prefect."

"It's bribery," said Katie. "Hooper's way of getting people to stay on. Everyone knows she gets more money, for every sixth former. So they get this reward, being a prefect. And that looks good on their college applications and things. It's all *corrupt*. You scratch my back, I'll scratch yours." Simultaneously, they burst into giggles, picturing Cleo Langham scratching Mrs. Hooper's back. "A little bit to the right, dear," gasped Katie, trying to do Mrs. Hooper's voice through her laughter. "Ah *that's* the spot! Oh bliss!"

And then the bell went, and they staggered through the north end main door, under the suspicious eye of the trio of prefects who guarded it from inside, in the warm.

As they headed for their own cloakroom, Gina sobered up. It was all very well for Katie to say that about Sharon not minding, but what about Lucy Connell? It wasn't as if Gina wasn't *involved*. Katie's high spirits and seemingly uncontrollable tongue often led to trouble, but it was generally very minor trouble. This might be serious. Cleo was sure to find out, sooner or later, and probably sooner, who Katie Walker was, or, more likely, who Sharon Vaughan was. She said something of this to Katie.

"Course she won't," said Katie. "And if she does, she won't remember. It'll be just a name, that she's given a detention to at some time. You know Cleo. By the end of every single day she's got a list of order marks and detentions long as your arm. They all blend into a sort of blur: filthy juniors. I bet she's given Sharon loads of order marks already. She said she knew the name; that'll be why. And she didn't remember that it wasn't me, did she? As long as nothing happens in the next day or two we're safe as anything. You worry too much, you do, Gina Bionic Window Cleaner."

"Um," said Gina, somewhat comforted. Katie was

probably right – she nearly always was. The only thing –
what if Sharon Vaughan, the real one, was to cross Cleo's
horrible path, within the next day or two, the danger
period? They hadn't any control over that, had they? Still, it
was a very big school, Compton Park... And Sharon was
more than likely off playing truant.

Their formroom was on the ground floor, just down the
corridor from the main hall. This had both good points and
bad. It meant you could be first in the queue for snacks at
break, and you didn't have to do the Great Trek every
morning to get to Assembly. The bad bit was that people
were always passing. You were Observed.

Cathy Mitchell was standing outside the door, which was
half open. "Watch it," she said. "Simon Dixon's just behind
the door, and he's pulling all the girls' skirts up as we go in."

"Ta," said Katie. "Amazing what some people'll do for
an eyeful of navy knicker. Retarded." She stepped forward
and gave the door a mighty kick. It flew back; there was a
howl. "Stupid sort of place to stand, innit, Dixon?" she said,
strolling in. "Get hurt, standing there." Roars of delight
from the class. Simon Dixon was clutching his funny bone;
he eyed Katie with loathing. "May as well have the leg to
match it," said Katie, and kicked him in the shin. Cheers of
derision. In came Miss Fleming.

"Will you all go to your seats *please*. Dixon, get up this
minute. You'll make the floor dirty. Now, I want everyone
to listen carefully, and the girls in particular." She perched
herself on the front of the table. Miss Fleming hated sitting
in her chair; she would wander around, lean against the
wall, balance herself on the chair arm; anything but sit in it.
"There's been another outbreak of this ridiculous
behaviour in the girls' toilets. *All* the toilets jammed up with
toilet rolls again. Shut up, Harper, that's not funny. Now,
I'm asking you for the last time. Does anybody in this form
know anything about it?" Silence. "I'm not suggesting

109

anyone here is responsible. I'm sure I know you better than that. But it's quite possible that you might know, or have a pretty good idea, just who is doing it. And it's essential that the culprits are caught. Mrs. Hooper doesn't see why anyone should have the bother of unblocking the toilets every night, so until further notice the toilets are out of bounds except during break and lunchtime, when there will be prefects there, supervising. During lesson-time they will be locked."

"Oh, Miss *Fleming*." Groans from all the girls. "But sometimes you *have* to go during a lesson."

"Thank you, Lindy, I hadn't finished. In cases of emergency you ask one of the staff for permission to use the sixth form toilets. Understood? Good. And you boys needn't look so pleased with yourselves. There have been plenty of incidents of vandalism in the boys' toilets, and Mrs. Hooper is quite prepared to introduce the same measures for you. So if anyone does know anything, they'd do well to report it. Otherwise everyone's going to suffer. Right. Now I'll take the register."

She did this standing, leaning against the wall, one foot resting on the pipes.

"That's a bit much," said Gina, to Katie. "Who on earth can be doing that? Sharon Vaughan?"

"Dunno. It's a bit mental, stuffing loo paper down toilets. Sharon's not mental. She hasn't said anything about it. If it was her she'd have got herself caught by now, probably. The whole point of what she's doing, is getting caught."

"Who then?"

"Perhaps that Michelle Wicks and her lot. You know, that Second Year with the fuzzy hair, got herself suspended last term. I reckon it might be her. They'll never find out. They'll keep this up for a few days, that's all. Then it'll be something else. I dunno though, Prefects in the bog. Imagine, nature calling like crazy, and Cleo Langham

110

outside, supervising. Instant constipation. Ugh."

"Bet that'll thrill them to death, though," said Gina. "Being stuck in the loos during break and all through lunch. They'll really enjoy that."

"Serve 'em right." said Katie. "Oh, heck, I haven't packed my stuff yet. What's first lesson? Oh, Maths. Good."

But first, out to Assembly, with prefects lining all the corridors and intersections, bawling their parrot-like cries: "Stop talking! Shut up! *Will* you stop talking?" The prefects made such a row that if they shut up themselves and left the rest of the school to it, the resulting noise would probably be no worse, thought Gina. If *she* ran a school she'd want it to be a happy place. This was like going to a daily early morning funeral. Dead Silence. What harm would a little quiet chatter do? Rules for the sake of rules.

When the holy bits were over Mrs. Hooper rose, majestically, to do her announcements. She announced, through her crackling microphone, that Mrs. Harrison would be leaving at the end of term. Ripples of indifference ran around the hall. They would, continued Mrs. Hooper balefully, be *very sorry to lose her*. Gina didn't even know who she was. So many teachers, and most of them you never had anything to do with at all. Grimly, Mrs. Hooper went on to repeat what Miss Fleming had said about the girls' toilets, and to give her opinion of such infantile behaviour. "And that is all I have to say. Stand!" Like the flipping army, stand, sit, turn. "Turn! And lead on." The school filed out, under the ever-watchful eyes of the prefects. And their mouths. "Shut up!" Stuart Burnford roared at Katie.

"But I didn't *say* anything," she complained, in the safety of the formroom. "I only got as far as opening my mouth. I might have been going to cough, or *breathe*, or something."

"No breathing in the corridors!" said Gina. Stuart Burnford was a giant-sized rat. He was the male equivalent

111

of Cleo Langham, except that he had the face to fit his character: a prize-fighter's mug, with a handful of nasty little pimples tastefully scattered. He and Cleo Langham were going out together. They were even rumoured to be getting engaged.

"Imagine what it'll be like for their kids, if they ever have any," Katie said, as they made their way to Room 5 and Maths. "They'll never let them in the house. 'Mummy, please can I come in for my tea?' 'No! Outside!'"

Gina giggled. "'Daddy, I'm so cold and it's nearly two in the morning, can't I please come in to bed?'" "'No!'" they chorused. "'Outside!'"

"They'll spend their entire married life," said Katie, "stationed one at the back door, one at the front, seeing that the kids don't get indoors..."

"Till one of them rings a bell..." This picture of the future Langham/Burnford ménage was almost unbearably funny; they half-collapsed into their desks.

"You two, you're always laughing at something," said Vicky Watts, somewhat enviously, turning round from the seat in front.

"I suppose we are," said Katie, weakly. "Oh dear..." and she was off again. Vicky waited, but, clearly, the joke was not to be explained to her; she shrugged, turned back, and proceeded to be very nasty indeed to her friend Julie, for being so dull and unamusing.

"Where's our Adam got to?" asked Katie. "How'm I supposed to overwhelm him with my womanly charms, when he doesn't even show up?"

"He was in Assembly," said Gina. "I saw him. Here he is now."

In bounded Mr. Billingham, with his mop-top and his long long legs. Just about every girl in 3F was, or had been, dreadfully in love with Mr. Billingham, despite the knowledge of the existence of a Mrs. Billingham, and two

112

little Billinghams. His charm was endless, and his lessons such fun. "Oh, I'm bored with base eight!" he would cry, and, hurling the book to the floor, would proceed to write a series of weird symbols on the board – "and there's a prize for the first one to work out the next two in the series." Or sometimes he would write out a problem on the board, always with a catch; like the one where train A leaves London for Glasgow travelling at 60 mph and half an hour later train B leaves Glasgow for London travelling at 80 mph, which train is nearer to London when they meet? And, he would add mischievously, give the date of the birth of *both* the drivers. Always there was a prize for the winner, generally a boiled sweet, though this caused problems; the most frequent winner was Mandy Lester, and she was diabetic and couldn't have sweets. So Mr. Billingham would pick up a piece of chalk, or extract a wilting flower from the vase on the table, and present it to her with a bow. You couldn't help but enjoy Maths, however hopeless you might be at it. Katie was more hopeless than almost anybody, and it was her favourite lesson. There was one more point in Mr. Billingham's favour, a very good point; he thought the prefects a terrific joke. "*Ja, mein Kommandant!*" he had been heard to murmur, after speaking to one. It was very endearing.

They worked quite hard for the first half hour. Then Mr. Billingham got bored with right-angled triangles, seized the chalk and quickly drew a football league table with certain figures missing. "Deduce the missing numbers," he said, gleefully. "A super Electrolux washing machine for the winner."

"A flippin' humbug, you mean."

"Do I detect a note of disbelief in your dulcet tones? Come on now, Katie, surprise us all. Stun us. Look here. Team B drew *all* their matches. That's the big giveaway."

"Is it?" said Katie, blankly. Peter Farmer won in the end.

Mandy Lester didn't finish it at all, but then, she was looking a bit seedy, today.

They had English next. Five minutes before the end of the lesson, Katie whispered: "D'you want to use the toilets, at break?"

"Yup."

"Me too. So let's run like mad and get there quick, 'cos there'll be an awful queue." Standing in queues was not suited to Katie's nature. As soon as the bell went, they charged.

"What if it's Cleo?"

"If it's Cleo," said Katie, "then we burst." But there, propped against the washbasins in a resigned sort of way, was Judy Lever. They liked Judy; they knew her from last year's school play, which they'd all been involved in.

"Dear dear," said Katie, shaking her head in sorrow. "Caught in the act. The phantom toilet roll fiend of Compton Park. I'm afraid I'll have to report this, Judy, to the highest authority . . ."

"Cheeky monkey," said Judy, tweaking her ear. "Honestly. What a way to spend break. If I knew who was doing this I'd kick them from here to Thursday fortnight. Oh, by the way, d'you remember I asked you to ask round your form for people to help with scenery for this year's play? I don't suppose by any miracle you found someone?"

"Oh *yes*," said Gina. "Katie went round and told everyone how much time they'd get off lessons, if they helped. I've got a great list of people for you."

"Really? That's marvellous. I was getting quite desperate, I was. Come on, then, where is it?"

"In my formroom," said Gina.

"She gets me a list, and she leaves it in her formroom." Judy raised her eyes to heaven. "I could do with it today . . . are you first or second dinner?"

"Second."

"Good – could you bring it to me at twelve fifteen, then? In the hall, say."

"Yeah, OK." People were beginning to arrive; they disappeared into the cubicles.

"Aw Judy," said Katie, all finished and hands, lingeringly, washed. "You aren't really going to throw us out into the sub-arctic, are you?"

"'Fraid I've got to," said Judy. "*Much* as it goes against the grain, laying down the law all over the place. No option."

"Do you *like* being a prefect, Judy?"

"You're joking. Petty officialdom and silly rules and doing the staff's dirty work for them. And it eats huge great chunks out of your free time."

"Can't you say no?"

"Refuse to be a prefect? Now you're *really* joking. The world would end. And my prospects with it. Now, stop trying to distract me, when I'm supposed to be throwing you out."

"I'll have a nervous breakdown," said Katie, "like that First Year, Julia whatsit."

"That'll be the day. You've got nerves of cast iron. And there's a rule about Third Years having breakdowns. It's definitely forbidden."

"Especially in the corridors," said Gina.

"Out!" said Judy. They gave in. Well, they'd used up a nice lot of break. As they left another two prefects arrived, to give Judy some rather belated support.

"Why are prefects like 98a buses?" asked Katie, and answered it herself: "They go around in threes, and they're almost totally empty on top."

"Except you never have to wait half an hour for one," said Gina. "They're always *there*."

"I wonder what gets into them, really." They were circling the Science Block again, stamping and shivering.

115

"This power mania that seems to take over. I mean, they must remember what it was like when *they* were lower school and the prefects were beastly to *them*. You'd think they'd be more – enlightened."

"Yes, well, it obviously doesn't work like that, does it? I suppose they get their revenge, only they get it on the wrong people. And the whole thing just goes on and on."

"Perpetuates itself," said Katie, who was good with words. "Well, I don't want to end up like that. I'm not having *my* beautiful character warped. That's a very good reason for leaving after the fifth year. Not that I wouldn't anyway."

"Um," said Gina; she knew full well that she herself would most certainly not be allowed to leave at sixteen. Her parents would go berserk if she even suggested it. She did wish Katie wasn't so determined to leave. They could have such fun in the sixth. They could be the first nice prefects in the history of the world. Well, apart from Judy. She mustn't forget that list.

Next lesson was History (Wars of the Roses) in their formroom with Miss Fleming; Gina got the list from her desk and put it in her satchel. Then off to Room 2I for Geography (glaciers). Only Mr. Morgan wasn't there. After five minutes the usual "Have you seen him today?" began; shortly afterwards in came a teacher, one of the new young ones, with a pile of green exercise books.

"Mr. Morgan's not here," she said, "so I'm sitting with you. Just get on with something quietly." This made her position clear; she was saying, "you keep the noise down to a gentle buzz and let me get on with my marking and I don't care if you do Geography or the football pools." 3F nodded in approval. Katie got a book out, more for show than because she intended reading it. Gina considered, then pulled out her drawing pad. She was in a drawing mood.

Drawing was Gina's great talent. People often wondered

116

what Katie, witty sharp comical Katie, saw in someone so quiet and unKatie-like as Gina. This was foolish. Every comic needs a straight man – or woman – and in any case Gina had a strong and quirky sense of humour of her own. She expressed it in her drawing, which mostly took the form of cartoons. She could draw anybody – cruel caricature, instantly recognizable. Katie would sigh with envy; to her, this was a good deal cleverer, and funnier, than anything she could do or say. The two of them set each other off perfectly, their friendship was rock solid.

"Do Cleo," Katie hissed now. Gina nodded. She had intended to do Cleo, lots of Cleos. She experimented first with a trio of double decker bus Cleos, travelling in convoy, but this was difficult, and would need to be worked on at length. She took a new sheet and drew Cleo and Stuart standing grimly before their front door, and a little row of freezing, imploring children, the youngest in a pram. "No! Outside!" she printed at the bottom. Then she did the same scene again, at night, Stuart in pyjamas, Cleo in curlers, children half buried in a snowdrift. Oh, this was fun, this was the life. Gina wanted more than anything to be a cartoonist. She couldn't imagine being happy doing anything else. But her parents wanted her to be a doctor. Trouble ahead. Gina tried not to think of it. She drew Cleo with sub-machine gun opening fire on a group of First Years; Cleo in SS uniform with swastika armband, standing in front of a mirror and trying on a Hitler moustache.

"Oh, Gina, that's absolutely brill." The lesson was over; only now did Katie dare to look, in case she couldn't swallow down her laughter. "God, if they printed those in the school magazine. How much better than the Annual Report of the History Society. Keep them safe. We'll publish them one day. I'll write the words."

"I do keep them," said Gina, stuffing them into her bag. "I've kept them all. Oh heck – the list! I'll have to run." She

117

tore off at breakneck speed. Katie followed at a more leisurely pace, depositing her bag in the formroom before strolling along to the hall. As she approached she saw Cleo Langham, clearly preparing for another stint of duty, warming up her vocal cords with a few gentle shrieks before moving on to the heavy stuff. Gina and Judy were leaning against one of the tables, apparently deep in conversation. Katie thought it prudent not to linger, not with Cleo on the rampage. She'd better wait outside. Where was all this snow then? You could never believe a word they said, those weather forecasters.

"Took your time," she grumbled, when Gina eventually emerged.

"Sorry. She went all through the list, wanted to know who'd be actually helpful and who'd just mess around." They began to pace up and down. A whole horrible half hour before they could go in to dinner, lovely warm dinner. The icy hard ground froze their feet; feet were the first to go, then hands and noses.

"And then I ... oh hell's bells."

"What?"

"I left my satchel there, didn't I. On the table. And – oh my God Cleo's on duty."

"So?"

"Well, she's not likely just to leave it there, is she? A satchel in the hall?" It wasn't like Katie to be so slow. "She'll pick it up, won't she, and have a look inside to see whose it is, and what's the first thing she'll see? The cartoons."

"Oh strewth." That, thought Gina, was putting it very mildly. "Look, don't *panic*."

"There's nothing else to do," said Gina, panicking.

"Yes there is. Just go in, right, and say you've left your satchel, by mistake, when you were talking to Judy – make a point of that, you were only there at all because a prefect sent for you – and she'll probably just say, get it and get out. No harm done. Look, Gina, you've *got* to. I can't go, I'm supposed to be avoiding her. You've got to. Think what'll happen if you don't."

Gina thought of it. She gulped, turned and went. She almost walked into Cleo. She repeated exactly what Katie had told her to say. "Too bad," said Cleo. "You'll just have to leave it there, won't you, and perhaps you won't be so careless another time. Any excuse to sneak indoors. I'll take charge of it. You can collect it from me before afternoon registration. Now buzz off. Nobody needs a satchel to eat their dinner. Get outside."

And that was that.

"She's only got to lift the flap," Gina said despairingly, "and it wasn't fastened, I know it wasn't, 'cos I'd just taken the list out of it."

"We have to get it," said Katie. "At once. Now, let's think. All legal entrances guarded by prefects. Windows unreachable. No chimneys to do the Santa Claus bit. So what's left?"

"We *could* dig a tunnel," said Gina, with sarcasm. There was no need for Katie to *enjoy* this. It wasn't her bag.

"Staff door," said Katie. "It's the only way. Don't look like that. It's the only door not guarded. And any of the staff who go home for dinner, or go out or anything, should have gone by now. It should be dead quiet."

"Should be." Gina didn't like it. The staff entrance, and all that side of the school, where they parked their cars, was out of bounds. And so *many* teachers using it. They would almost certainly be caught. And yet – it was ideally situated. The staff door led into a little lobby, which led in turn directly into the main hall. She imagined Cleo, looking at those cartoons. They had to try.

"Attagirl," said Katie. They made their way around the side of the building, pressing tightly against the wall until

119

the point where the drive swung away to pass through a sort of shrubbery. Gina was shaking and queasy with nerves. It was so menacingly quiet here, and at any moment a car might charge round the corner – it might be Mrs. *Hooper's* car . . .

"All clear," whispered Katie. And then stopped. Stopped dead. And pointed dumbly. There was a body in the shrubbery.

It was a couple of feet back from the drive, between two bushy plants. Passing in a car you probably wouldn't even notice it. Katie stepped forward. "Oh Lord," she said. "It's Mandy."

"*Mandy?*" Gina rushed to her side; an anonymous body was quite a different thing from a body that was Mandy – though which was worse? "Oh, Katie, she isn't dead?"

"Course she's not *dead*," said Katie angrily; at first she had thought so, and that moment of helpless disbelieving numbing horror was not something she would easily forget. "She's in a coma, isn't she?" They all knew about the danger of comas for a diabetic, but they'd never seen Mandy in one before. "But if she's not moved from here soon she will be. It's flippin' perishing. She'll get pneumonia . . ." Katie moved to lift Mandy, who was lying on her side. She'd hit her face when she fell; it was scratched and bleeding. Then she hesitated. She'd always thought you shouldn't move unconscious people – and she didn't really know a thing about diabetes, there might be something you had to do to someone in a coma before you moved them – they might kill her . . . "We'd better get Mrs. Ross," she said. "Come on!" They ran, hell for leather, round the final bend of the drive, up to the staff door and inside, through the lobby, flung open the door to the hall – and there, as if waiting for them, stood Cleo Langham.

"Now you've *really* done it. Persistent disobedience, *and* out of bounds. I'm reporting this to Mrs. Hooper."

"Cleo, get out of the way, you stupid nurd, there's a girl out there in a *coma*..."

Cleo didn't budge. Her body blocked the entrance; she spread her legs to prevent a possible dash round the side, and to anchor herself more firmly. "Oh come on, you can do better than that. I've had one already pretending she was going to pass out. She was *much* more convincing than you. You could use her in the school play ... what the hell d'you think you're doing?" Katie had already done it. She had dived through Cleo's legs, and was even now rolling to her feet on the other side. "I don't believe it..."

"Run, Katie," shouted Gina, and pushed past Cleo into the hall. Katie was already at the staff room door; as she raised her hand to knock, it opened, and out came Mr. Billingham – dear, wonderful Mr. Billingham. He looked down enquiringly at Katie from the lofty heights of his six foot three.

"Mandy," said Katie. "She's lying in the shrubbery, in a coma."

"Right," said Mr. Billingham, and disappeared back inside at speed. Seconds later, Mrs. Ross (Games) appeared, Mr. Billingham at her heels.

"These two," said Mr. Billingham, indicating Katie and Gina.

"Come on," said Mrs. Ross, "show me where she is. Hurry. Out of the *way*, Cleo." They all ran outside, Cleo following at a distance.

"Let's get her indoors," said Mrs. Ross, checking for Mandy's pulse. Mrs. Ross had gone quite pale. "Maureen's phoned for an ambulance. The poor child." She picked Mandy up with as much ease as if she were a kitten. Cleo sidled forward, her face registering something like alarm.

"Oh Cleo," said Katie. "This must be the girl who told you she was going to pass out, and you didn't believe her. How awful."

For a moment nobody said anything. Then Mrs. Ross paused and asked: "Is this true, Cleo?"

"They try so many excuses," Cleo said faintly.

"How long ago?"

"Five – maybe ten minutes."

Mrs. Ross just looked at her. A look that said more than words ever could. Then she marched off, carrying Mandy's inert body.

"Cleo," said Mr. Billingham. "In future I think it would be as well if you were to temper your vigilance with a *little* common sense."

Cleo bit her lip, turned and walked back inside. The others followed. Back in the hall, Katie drew Gina aside, and pointed. "Your satchel, look. Go get it."

Gina looked quickly at Mandy, who had roused a little, muttered something and lapsed back into unconsciousness. Well, it wasn't going to make any difference to Mandy, was it, if she got her satchel out of Cleo's clutches. She picked it up and went off to dump it in the formroom.

Katie pulled at Mr. Billingham's sleeve. "She is going to be all right, isn't she?"

"I hope so." He looked rather shaken, himself. Mandy's face was almost waxen, now, under those cuts. Katie realized that the cuts probably weren't nearly so bad as they looked.

"She'll be all right," said Mrs. Ross. "If she was on her feet and talking to Cleo ten minutes ago, there shouldn't be any lasting damage. Where's that ambulance? I suppose she made her way around to the staff entrance thinking that was the only place she was likely to be taken seriously." She gave Cleo another look. Cleo moved away. "Ah, good, here they are now." She stepped forward to speak to the ambulance men. "I'll go with her," she said. "Has someone notified the parents?"

"Maureen said she'd ring them," said Mr. Billingham.

Katie wondered vaguely who Maureen might be. The ambulance men – one of them was a woman – lifted Mandy on to a stretcher-thing, and covered her with red blankets; the ambulance party moved off.

"Awful thing, diabetes," Mr. Billingham said to Katie, and to Gina, who had just returned. "I suppose she's either not had her insulin for some reason, or had the insulin but not enough food to go with it. Either way, you go into a coma. Awful. Friend of my sister's has it. Now you two." He was sounding more like his proper self. "For the life of me I can't imagine what you were doing in the shrubbery. But it's extremely fortunate that you were, isn't it?"

"Extremely," said Katie.

"So I think perhaps not too many questions will be asked . . . you did very well, to act so promptly. Not panicking."

"I nearly panicked," said Gina. "She looked so . . ."

"Dead," said Katie, never one to mince words. She was thinking – couldn't help thinking – *if* Gina hadn't done the cartoons, *if* Judy hadn't asked for the list today, *if* Gina hadn't forgotten her bag, *if* Cleo had let her fetch it, then they *wouldn't* have been in the shrubbery, and Mandy *would* be . . . no. They'd never know. One of the staff might have driven past seconds later, and seen her. It was, Katie decided, *more* than likely. And, meanwhile, here was Cleo again, coming their way. To apologize perhaps?

"Mr. Billingham?"

"Katie?"

"Seeing as we did so well and acted so promptly and didn't panic, and Mandy being one of your best pupils and all, would you do us a big favour? When Cleo gets here would you call me Sharon and Gina Lucy?"

Mr. Billingham looked perplexed. "Certainly not, Sharon," he said as Cleo came to a halt behind them. "Out of the question, Lucy. And now I really must get back to my once piping hot tea and my Embassy Slim Panatella. If you care to come and see me after school I'll let you know what news we have from the hospital."

Exit Mr. Billingham, inscrutably. Katie and Gina turned to face Cleo. Cleo glowered. Her face said all sorts of things. But her mouth produced one word only.

"Outside!"

ROCK OF AGES

Annabel was talking on the phone to her friend Vanessa. When they had finished, Vanessa would ring Carla, who would ring Marina, who might well ring Annabel, completing the circle. These telephone conversations would touch on one subject only. Annabel had an appointment for four o'clock. She was taking the plunge. Annabel was going to have herself Done.

"You're so *brave*," said Vanessa for the seventh time. "I do wish I dared. But my Mum'd go mad. Won't your Dad go mad? I'd have thought he'd hit the roof."

"Probably he will," said Annabel bravely; more bravely than she felt. "But it'll be too late, then, to do anything about it. And I expect he'll come round in the end." Annabel was her father's pride and joy, the light of his life; for thirteen years she had been successfully twisting him around her little finger. Or whichever finger she pleased.

"You're so brave," said Vanessa.

"Oh, I don't know," said Annabel generously. "You're the one who's been using the Wrinkle Cream, after all. How long is it now? A fortnight? Have you noticed any difference?"

"Twelve days," said Vanessa, "and I think perhaps it's

starting to work. Things do seem to be happening to my neck. I'll show you this afternoon. What time are we meeting? Three?"

"Three, yeah. Outside Marks and Sparks. You tell Carla, then."

"*So* brave," said Vanessa with a mournful sigh, and rang off.

The 17.35 train was six minutes late leaving Victoria.

"Six minutes!" said Mr. Potter to Mr. Gilling.

"Six!" said Mr. Gilling. They unfolded their *Standards* as the train rolled over the points, clickety clack, southward bound. When they reached Limmington Junction they would refold their papers and spend the last fifteen minutes of their journey having a nice discussion about the terrible state of the world. Mr. Gilling and Mr. Potter were mostly of one mind. They disapproved of everything. The world was decaying before their very eyes. It was all most enjoyable.

"Limmington Junction," said Mr. Potter, some twenty-five minutes later. He waited for Mr. Gilling to make the first move.

"Ah," said Mr. Gilling. And then: "I sometimes wonder." This was the standard opener. "I sometimes wonder, Potter, if after the punks died out, all the young people in this country got together and said, now, let's see what we can think of that will shock them even more than the punks. Something un*think*ably vile. And by God, Potter, they've succeeded. They've succeeded. It's unspeakable. Gerries! Disgusting! An insult to our Senior Citizens! Look over there." He pointed to an elderly lady, dozing, mouth open, three seats away. "Is she real? Or is she a Gerry? Potter..." he said with anguish – "...you can't tell the difference any more!"

"Shocking!" said Mr. Potter, with relish. "Of course, it's

merely the latest manifestation of the old gang instinct. The urge to identify with the group." Potter fancied himself as a sociologist. "That's why they all dress alike. Terribly primitive, really. Absolutely tribal. And the need to shock their elders. Rebellion against the Parent Figure."

"My little Annabel," said Mr. Gilling, mournfully, tenderly. "Of course I've had to give up Michael as a bad job. The boy is beyond my control. He has bought himself a Bender, Potter!"

"*Not* the Bender!"

"The Bender. Curve Your Own Spine. I could weep, Potter. My son is turning himself into a hunchback and I am helpless – helpless to stop it. Where will it end? Of course," he added venomously, "it's all that woman's fault!"

"That vile woman," agreed Mr. Potter.

"Even my little Annabel. Obsessed by her. Pictures and posters all over her bedroom wall. I tell you, Potter, I used to go quite regularly to an Old People's Home to visit my Auntie Dorothy, now safely God rest her soul in the hands of the Almighty. And the sight that always hit you when you walked through the door was this: a large room, a television in the corner, and, all around the walls, old ladies. Little old ladies, in chairs, clinging to the walls. And it's exactly like that now in Annabel's room. Television in the corner, and plastered all over the walls, little old ladies. All of them the same little old lady. It's terrifying. And the mask! Everywhere you look, the mask."

"Masked Granny," said Potter. "The original bad apple. She has rotted the entire youth of your nation."

"Rotten to the core!" Mr. Gilling said viciously. He was well acquainted with the history of the Masked Granny phenomenon. His children talked of little else. Their reading matter now consisted entirely of Masked Granny Weekly, Masked Granny's Christmas Special, The Masked

Granny Guide to the Geriatric Lifestyle. Michael, who had once been a healthy science fiction addict. Little Annabel, who seemed so recently to have been enjoying Paddington Bear. Now – Looking Old, Feeling Ancient, by Masked Granny.

It had all begun little more than a year ago with the release of Masked Granny's first single, 'I'm so Old (I'm Falling to Pieces)'. This was a timely event. The previous youth craze, Scudge Music, had died away. Former Scudge musicians swelled the dole queues. This caused a serious recession in the Teenage Exploitation industry. A new cult must be established as soon as possible – for what use were teenagers to anyone, if they could not be parted from their money? It wouldn't do!

There were several false starts and flat shots. The Pseudo-Classical movement, which, it was claimed, would be bigger than punk, would make the Liverpool sound appear a mere hiccup in the history of music by comparison. It died an instant death and was promptly forgotten. There was a brief experiment in which five-year-old children were dressed as Teds to sing reggae versions of Gilbert and Sullivan. For some reason this didn't work either. There was Monotone. Monotone meant that a group dressed entirely in one colour – say green – and with their hair, faces and hands dyed green, would come out on to a green set, pick up their green guitars and perform a song consisting of one single note, repeated ad infinitum. The speed, length and volume of the notes could of course be varied, though this was held to be against the true spirit of Monotone. Monotone flopped.

It may have been a stroke of genius, or pure chance, that solved the problem. The truth of the origins of the Masked Granny phenomenon has been lost in the mists of legend. What is known beyond doubt is that one Thursday, on *Top of the Pops*, a little old lady wheeled herself on to the stage, gave a sudden howl, stood up and began to scream the now universally known lyrics of 'I'm so Old (I'm Falling to Pieces)'. In between the choruses she destroyed the entire set, and seriously injured a bouncer. The performance was received with rapture. Everyone knew that something rather special had happened.

The Masked Granny industry seemed to arise overnight. Suddenly she was everywhere. Within a week of that initial momentous appearance, her first album, *Thoughts of a Geriatric Ghoul*, was released. Even at this early stage her followers were beginning to call themselves Gerries.

Perhaps the key to her freak success was the sheer mystery surrounding the woman. Who was she? *Why* was she? Nobody knew. The mask was never lifted one single millimetre. All that anyone knew about her was that she was little, prone to violence, had some remarkably nasty habits and was very, very old. Even the source of her songs was a mystery. She rarely gave interviews. She was surrounded at all times by a protective circle consisting of her manager, four bodyguards, three roadies and a Dobermann Pinscher. It was rumoured that Masked Granny herself was potentially more lethal than any two of these combined. Thus was her privacy preserved.

And the nation loved her. Suddenly Old Age was In. It was fashionable. "Youth and old age are both symptoms of the same malignant disease," said Masked Granny gleefully, in one of her infrequent quotes. The Old Look began to appear on the streets. Boutiques were hastily stocked with long johns and combinations. There was a resurgence of the cami-knicker, and even the whalebone corset. It was unthinkable to be seen at a disco without your wheelchair.

The centre of the revolution, the eye of the hurricane, Masked Granny herself, cackled wickedly and released her second single, a double A-side, 'Meals on Wheels/Towards the Grave'. It went straight to Number One and remained there for eight weeks. From being – well, from being whoever she was – Masked Granny had risen to the very pinnacle of fame. Her name cropped up in the House of Commons whenever pensions were debated. (Masked Granny took personal credit for the 13.5% increase in pensions announced in October.) Every self-respecting impressionist had to include Masked Granny in his or her repertoire. She was named as Worst Dressed Woman of the Year. There were Masked Granny Lookalike contests, and a nationwide Find Masked Grandpa competition. (It is said that when the winner of this was presented to Masked Granny, she kicked him in the groin.)

Mr. Gilling was by no means alone in his predicament. Parents in their hundreds of thousands had watched their children fall victim to the charms – charms? – of this most unlikely of pop stars. Nonetheless, Mr. Gilling took it personally. *Both* his children. It was too much. He felt that Masked Granny had it in for him. She was a demon, a midnight hag, an unholy witch. The polluter of his Annabel.

When he got home, neither of his children was in. He never knew, these days, whether to be sorry or relieved at this. On the whole he thought he was relieved. It meant he needn't start shouting straight away. He could have a nice relaxing sit first.

It was, then, most irritating to discover that his wife had a guest, and a stranger at that. An old woman. At first he'd thought it was his mother. He stood, polite but weary, waiting to be introduced.

"Hello, Daddy," said the old woman.

Mr. Gilling went quite white. He groped for a chair. He missed. He began to tremble.

"Let me help you, dear," said his wife, rushing to the rescue. "There you are. Oh, Annabel, see what you've

130

done! You've really frightened your father. Come on, Brian. Bear up."

"*Ann*abel," said Mr. Gilling, feebly. He glanced quickly at his mother – his daughter – and hastily averted his eyes. It was too horrible. It was a nightmare.

"Annabel went to the Merry Gerry Salon this afternoon," said Mrs. Gilling.

"You ... you *knew*." His own wife, betraying him.

"Of course I didn't know, dear. I had no idea. But it's done now, and can't be undone. You have to face it, Brian. This is still Annabel. Still your daughter. Appearances aren't everything; it's the person inside that one cares for."

Rubbish, thought Mr. Gilling. Twaddle. Bunk. "*What* has she had done?" he asked. It was better to know. As long as he wasn't expected to look. He would never look at her again.

"Just my hair," Annabel said cheerfully. "Greyed and thinned ..."

"Thinned!"

"... and the Wrinkle Treatment. Not all over, Daddy, really. Only the bits that show. And the Granny glasses, of course. It's a waste of money being Done if you don't have the glasses."

"You have perfect eyesight. What's she going to do?" – he turned to his wife in sudden desperation. He couldn't yet bring himself to address Annabel directly. "She can't go to school looking like that. This is the end of her education. Oh God!"

"Daddy, don't be silly! We've just broken up, remember? No school for six weeks. And the grey and the wrinkles will have faded by then," she added, not without regret. "It's only a Temporary. I couldn't afford a Permanent."

"Permanent!" said Mr. Gilling, almost in tears. Annabel's spirits rose. He'd feel ever so much better if he had a good cry. It was just as well, she thought, that he didn't know about her other purchases. Her tube of Wrinklina Wonder, the Instant Wrinkle Cream, brand new on the market. No more waiting twelve days for things to start happening to your neck. Vanessa's neck was coming along nicely, but Annabel simply didn't have that sort of patience. With the Wrinklina she could touch up the Temporary when it began to wear off. And she had a set of Masked Granny poison-tipped knitting needles, with matching exploding three-ply baby wool balls, the sort Masked Granny threw at the audience during her concerts. She wouldn't tell her father about those, either.

"Thinned," said Mr. Gilling, miserably. "Thinned. That lovely hair, the colour of ripe corn. Now she's grey and half bald!"

"It'll grow back, dear," said Mrs. Gilling, consolingly.

"It'll be the *wrong length*."

"Not necessarily the *wrong* length. Just – different from the rest. Like being layered. Very attractive, that." The back door banged.

"Here's Michael," said Annabel. Her father uttered a sound that might have been "yaargh". They listened to the heavy footsteps approaching, slow, slow, painfully slow. The door opened; in shuffled Michael, pushing his walking frame before him. Hunched and crooked. Annabel watched in open admiration. That Bender was really good. It had worked miracles on Michael's back. He looked really *old*. She must try to borrow the Bender, some time.

Michael hobbled agonizingly to a chair, and lowered himself gingerly into it. Only then did he look up and see his sister.

"Annabel!"

"Yeah?" said Annabel. This was the confrontation she'd been *really* nervous about. Michael was an expert. He could judge. If Michael didn't like it she'd have wasted her money. And she'd feel such a fool . . .

132

"That is . . ."

"Yes?"

"That is fantastic! That is really, really *old*, Annabel. You look about ninety!"

"Honest? You're not just saying that?"

"Course not. It's terrif." It was astounding. He'd never have thought she had it in her – little baby Annabel, Daddy's girl, soppy date – and now look at her. Really geriatric. He'd be quite pleased to be seen with her if only she wasn't his sister. "What d'you reckon, Dad?" Not that he needed to ask. He knew very well what his dad would reckon.

"An abomination," said Mr. Gilling. He was recovering. Slightly. "A total abomination. This is the darkest day of my life. I doubt that I shall ever be the same again." Michael looked pleased at this. "Living with two . . . two . . . *Gerries*." He uttered the hated word with a sort of a spit. "Those stupid Granny glasses! I wonder you don't both get the mask as well and be done with it."

"*Daddy!*" said Annabel, shocked. Michael groaned. "Only Masked Granny wears the mask!" They looked at him accusingly, as if he had committed blasphemy. "You *know* that, Daddy," said Annabel.

Of course he knew. He knew all the rules. He heard them five times a day. Oh – he couldn't bear it. He couldn't. He would pass away in the night. Annabel – his little girl. He remembered, with a painful vividness, how as a tiny tot she used to say: "*Love* you, Daddy" and stick her dear little finger up his nose. His heart had melted every time. And now – a monster. Hideous. An obscenity.

"Oh, Brian, it's really not all that bad," said Mrs. Gilling, seeing his expression. "We've been brainwashed in this society, you know, to think young is beautiful. Well, I don't know." Mr. Gilling sniffed. She sounded like Potter. "I think this Old Look is quite attractive, Brian. One must

133

try to look at it with unconditioned eyes. What is so wonderful about smooth skin? Wrinkles and folds are so much more interesting." Mr. Gilling shuddered, remembering his glimpse of Annabel, crow's feet round her eyes, scraggy neck looking like the surface of the moon, her young features creased and wrinkled and lined ... that pitiful grey frizz on top... "After all," his wife continued, "I'm sure if I had to choose between a view of flat scenery, level and even as far as you can see, like Holland, and somewhere like the Alps, all valleys and mountains and ridges and exciting little twists and turns – I know which *I'd* choose. I know which most people would choose. And it's the same with faces. A weathered face has so much more – character. And grey – such a very refined colour, I always think. You must try to see both sides of it, Brian. This youth-worship cult we've had for so long is positively unhealthy. Everyone battling all their lives to try to stay looking young – a vain battle – when really it's entirely natural to age. Now young people are trying to look old. I think it's all very exciting. It could bring about a *drastic* change in the attitudes of society. No more treating the old like cast-offs, second class citizens. No more..."

"I don't care!" said Mr. Gilling. "Annabel looks like a freak! That is what *I* care about. She looks like nothing on the face of this earth! She doesn't look human!"

"Nonsense, dear," said Mrs. Gilling, kindly. "She looks *exactly* like your mother."

"Ten minutes!" said Potter as the 17.35 slowly gathered speed. "Thursday always seems to be a bad day."

"Every day is a bad day," said Mr. Gilling. Potter nodded, with understanding. He had heard the whole sorry tale on the morning train. It was all great fun. There were few things Potter enjoyed so much as other people's misfortunes.

134

Mr. Gilling lowered his head to the *Standard*. On Page Two was a large item – with photo – about Masked Granny's forthcoming tour of the Home Counties. He wouldn't read it. He wouldn't read *anything*. The woman was probably lurking on every page. She had found out that he read the *Standard* and had done it deliberately to spite him. He tried to think of something cheering. It took a long time. Eventually he remembered that there was a repeat of the BBC *Macbeth* being shown tonight. That was something. He would like that. Although – suddenly, appalled, he pictured the three witches – masked – sitting round their cauldron, and "Double, double, toil and trouble, fire burn and cauldron bubble" melted into:

> *I'm so old, I'm falling to pieces,*
> *All my skin is lines and creases.*
> *If I was a horse they'd have shot me*
> *But I'm just an old, old lady, so you've still got me . . .*

rendered in Masked Granny's inimitable scream.

"Limmington Junction!" said Potter. "Well, Gilling, I see the old bat is going on tour. Very strenuous, I should have thought. For someone her age. It may well kill her."

"Let us cling to that hope," said Mr. Gilling, with feeling.

"Your children are certain to want to go."

"They shan't go! If I have to lock them indoors for a week, they shan't go. I've heard what that woman does to her audiences." Potter had taken out one of his blue notebooks and was idly scribbling. This was a habit of his. Potter was something very Senior in the Civil Service. Mr. Gilling, who wasn't nearly so senior, knew better than to ask questions.

"I certainly shouldn't let them go," said Potter, looking up.

"You're so lucky, not to have children, Potter."

"Yes, I know," said Potter, and chuckled. "I was just

reading about a boy in Manchester, went to his dentist and begged her to pull out all his teeth so he could wear his Masked Granny Dentures. She threw them at him, you see, at a concert."

"Umph," said Mr. Gilling, picturing Annabel with a fractured skull, caused by the impact of one of Masked Granny's foul artificial molars. These denture-hurling sessions were a regular feature of her concerts. The removal of the dentures seemed to affect the quality of her singing not at all. The train stopped at Woodford Grove. An old man climbed in. Mr. Gilling regarded him with suspicion. There were no seats available. Nobody moved. Nobody offered him a seat. Was he, or wasn't he? "You see?" said Mr. Gilling. "That is typical. That is happening all over the country, every single day, Potter. No respect for the elderly any more. No consideration."

"I don't remember any respect for the elderly," said Potter. "Semi-senile old nuisances, outlived their usefulness, always moaning and grumbling that things weren't what they used to be. *That*, as I recall, was the common attitude towards the elderly. You must see both sides of the coin, Gilling. Mugging, theft and violent assault on the elderly have practically died out. The thugs are too scared. *They* can't tell the difference either. That doddering old man might be a healthy lad of eighteen. And with all this self-defence they teach them at school nowadays ... remarkable, really. Every cloud has its silver lining."

"Bosh," said Mr. Gilling, rising and straightening his coat. "You sound like my wife, Potter."

"Have a pleasant evening," said Potter.

"I shall endeavour to," said Mr. Gilling. "But I consider it unlikely. I shall distract myself by watching *Macbeth*."

"'Is that a dagger that I see before me?'" mused Potter, and poked Mr. Gilling playfully in the ribs. Mr. Gilling scowled. Potter wasn't himself, these days. He was becoming far too forward. He had taken to writing verse in his spare time. It was entirely out of character – Potter a poet! Potter, the last bastion of misery. But, in a world like this, it was probably only to be expected.

And the sight that greeted him when he opened the front door was only to be expected, as well. "What's this?" he said petulantly. His house was full of people. Teenage people. The very worst sort.

"It's Vanessa," said his wife brightly, "and Marina and Carla. They've come round to watch some programme with Annabel."

"No," said Mr. Gilling. "No, no, no. Not tonight. Please not. It's *Macbeth*!"

"What *do* you mean, Daddy?" asked Annabel.

Her father gazed at the wall. "I wanted to watch *Macbeth*," he said. "I have been looking forward to it *all day*," he added, untruthfully.

"Oh, but Daddy. I've invited all my friends round."

"I see that."

"Why didn't you say last night?"

"I was not capable of speech last night." The girls all giggled at that. He allowed himself to look at them. They appeared normal. They had not been Done. Why Annabel, and not them? "I suppose," he said heavily, "It's *Top of the Pops*." Masked Granny was bound to be Number One. She was always Number One.

"Not *only*. She's giving an *interview*. She's agreed to talk to Mark Tolland on *Lookaround*."

"Talking about the tour," said Vanessa, or was it Carla? Mr. Gilling winced at the mention of the tour. He hoped fervently that Annabel wasn't going to ask him about it now. There would be a Scene. He didn't think he could cope with a Scene, not in his present state.

"And we've worked out," said Annabel, "that if we turn over straight away we'll be in good time to see her on Top of the Pops. 'Senile Dementia/Brittle Bones' is still Number One, you see, Daddy."

"For the ninth successive week," said Carla (or Vanessa) reverently.

"Oh."

"But," Annabel said generously, "you can go and watch *Macbeth* on my TV if you like, Daddy. It wouldn't matter, that being in black and white. Not like it would with Masked Granny."

"I don't think so, thank you all the same." Macbeth. The immortal Bard, and all around, leering down from the walls, a thousand Masked Grannies. It would kill him.

"Brian!" called Mrs. Gilling. "Do come and have your dinner."

"What about *those*?" He jerked a thumb in the direction of Annabel and her friends.

"Oh, the girls and Michael and I have eaten already." Mrs. Gilling liked Annabel's friends. "Michael's gone to his Gerry Awareness meeting. Do hurry, dear. It's getting cold."

As he left the room Mr. Gilling heard one of the girls say: "Is your Dad's name really Brian? Isn't he *sweet*?" He didn't enjoy his dinner at all.

"I'll wash," said his wife when he had finished, "and you wipe. All right, dear?"

"Umph." Mr. Gilling hated wiping. He hated washing, too. As he rose, something on the sideboard caught his eye. "And what is *that*?"

"Masked Granny's new album," said Mrs. Gilling. "Marina brought it round. They're going to listen to it later. Annabel hasn't been able to afford it yet. The Merry Gerry Salon isn't exactly cheap."

"'I Can't Get no Putrefaction,'" read Mr. Gilling. "What? How *dare* she? The old witch! She's taking the mick out of the Rolling Stones!"

"Brian!" His wife had sidled to the mirror and was examining her reflection. "That's really quite funny! Taking the mick – Jagger, you see? A joke! I think that's the funniest thing you've said in the last ten years!"

"But ... the Stones..." His voice died away. There were no words to describe this latest outrage.

"You see?" said his wife blithely. "Nothing really changes. When you were a teenager you loved the Stones, and I'm sure your parents thought they were absolutely disgusting."

"There is no comparison," said Mr. Gilling stiffly. Briefly, painfully, he remembered those long ago days ... I can't get no satisfaction ... his hips gave a tiny, nostalgic wriggle. No! The past was past. "You seem to be finding that mirror very interesting," he said quickly.

"Mmmm ... you know, Brian ... it's very gratifying ... someone I met today took me for fifty! I swear to you. They simply refused to believe it when I said I was forty-four. 'You don't look a day under forty-eight', they..."

"You're thirty-nine!" screamed Mr. Gilling. "It's getting to you now! You're starting to lie about your age!" He went and stood behind her. Fifty? His Linda, his lovely Linda, mistaken for a woman of fifty? She didn't look more than ... she looked fifty.

"What have you been doing to yourself?" he roared.

"I thought you'd never notice," said his wife, pleased. "I've been trying this cream of Annabel's. Wrinklina Wonder, it's called. I simply wouldn't have believed it, such a difference in twenty-four hours..."

Mr. Gilling ran from the room. "Dear, dear," said his wife; and, turning to the empty room, conversationally: "I tell you what, then, I'll wash and I'll wipe. Fifty!" She was singing to herself as she squirted the Fairy Liquid.

Mr. Gilling entered the front room just in time to witness the entrance of Masked Granny. The girls were grouped round the television, rapt. The one he thought was Carla was trembling with suppressed emotion. Some unidentifiable force kept him in the room. "Know thine enemy," he thought, wondering if that was a genuine quote or if he had just made it up, all by himslf.

Masked Granny hobbled to her chair. She was dressed all in black, and carried a single knitting needle. This was very menacing. It was well known what damage Masked Granny could do with a knitting needle. Mark Tolland, the programme presenter, was clearly aware of this. He slid his chair back a couple of inches. Masked Granny promptly shuffled her chair towards him, with one of her famous leers. She was now closer than she had been in the first place.

Mark Tolland cleared his throat. "Masked Granny. Welcome to *Lookaround*. We're all so very pleased that you were able to join us."

"I'm sure you are," said Masked Granny. There was the sound offstage of a Dobermann Pinscher, barking.

"You are now, so to speak, at the very top of the tree. You are one of the most famous people in the country." Masked Granny did not deign to answer this. It was a self-evident truth. "What has all this success meant to you?"

"Money," said Masked Granny, chuckling. She began to bore a hole in the table with her knitting needle.

"If we could talk about your new album, which was released yesterday."

"It's very good," said Masked Granny. "It's brilliant. If the first one hadn't been perfect I'd say this one was even better. Everyone should buy one. I'm an old, old lady. Have you bought one?" she demanded suddenly, jabbing the needle at Mark.

"I've bought six," Mark said, wisely. Masked Granny nodded, made a purring noise, hurled her knitting needle at Tele-Cine Two, and produced another from within one of her black woollen stockings.

"Masked Granny," said Mark, clinging to these two words as if they were the only things he could be sure of in this uncertain world. "You must be aware that the whole world is wild to know who you really are. Your identity is the burning question of the moment. Will you give us just a hint?"

"Never," said Masked Granny. "The mask will never be removed. Not as long as I live. And I'm a very, very old lady, and can't be expected to live much longer, so everybody had better come to see me at one of my concerts on the forthcoming tour because they probably won't get another chance. I'm fading fast! I'm so old!" she suddenly screamed – "I'm falling to pieces!" This produced a sort of hysteria in the four girls in the Gillings' front room. "All my skin is lines and..." She broke off abruptly. "I'm bored now. I think I'll go home."

"Oh, no!" Mark felt near to panic. There were seven minutes of scheduled interview time left to fill, and she'd hardly said a thing yet. "*Please* don't go," he said, reaching over and laying a friendly, restraining hand on her arm. "Please don't..."

"Assault!" shrieked Masked Granny. There was immediate chaos. On to the set rushed a manager, four bodyguards, three roadies and a Dobermann Pinscher. Chairs and bodies flew. Blood was seen to collect in a scarlet pool on the studio floor. (The blood was later identified as belonging to Mark Tolland, who was subsequently hospitalized for six weeks.) Only then did the editor have the presence of mind to cut to another item, lined up on videotape.

There was a simultaneous expulsion of breath from all four girls. A release of almost unbearable tension. They had forgotten that Mr. Gilling was there. They had not heard his cries of "Vandal", "Obtuse old crone" and "Senile delinquent". They had been transported to a higher plane.

141

Marina was in tears. "Oh, Masked Granny," whispereed Annabel. There was no more to be said.

It was Vanessa who remembered *Top of the Pops*. There was a mad scramble to switch channels. It was the usual film; an extract from "Masked Granny at the Rainbow", an event which had caused a twenty-four-hour road-block to be set up in the Finsbury Park area. Mr. Gilling had seen it before. He knew the precise moment at which Masked Granny would begin to saw up her rocking chair, set it alight and fling it, piece by piece, at her delirious audience. He had seen the state of semi-hysterical ecstasy which this performance aroused in Annabel. He did not wish to witness this fourfold. He left the room.

He picked up the telephone. He would ring Thames Television and lodge a stern complaint about the outrageous scenes of violence on *Lookaround* that evening. He couldn't get through. He persevered for a quarter of an hour, and finally succeeded in obtaining a crossed line to Holloway prison. This seemed strangely meaningful. He went to bed, and dreamed that his wife had turned into his mother and insisted on calling him Daddy.

"I shall emigrate to Australia," said Mr. Gilling, as the 17.35 drew to a shuddering halt at Limmington Junction. It had been eight minutes late leaving Victoria.

"Oh, that won't do at all," said Potter. "They're planning to name a road after her in Perth. There's talk of a special performance in the Sydney Opera House. And anyway, Gilling, you don't like the heat."

"I shall go to Alaska," said Mr. Gilling, with less conviction.

"The Anchorage Gerries are already planning a pilgrimage to her spiritual birthplace, the *Top of the Pops* studio. And you don't like the cold."

"You seem very knowledgeable all of a sudden." Mr.

Gilling turned accusingly to face Potter. "Since when have you . . . Potter?"

"Gilling?"

"You . . . you're . . . your *face*." He very rarely had occasion to look directly at Potter. They preferred to stare in a depressed sort of way at the floor, littered as it was with cigarette ends and sniffed-out glue pots and other signs of degeneracy. "Potter, you've aged! You've aged ten years!"

"Do you really think so? How *very* gratifying," Potter said modestly. "I must admit that I've had a little help. A most excellent preparation." He withdrew a tube from his inside pocket. "Wrinklina Wonder. Remarkably efficacious. I would recommend . . ."

There was a thud as Mr. Gilling hit the floor. Amazing, thought Potter. Foaming at the mouth, he thought, spellbound. He did not summon help. He was not capable of doing so. Potter was a creative artist at the moment of inspiration, and was capable of nothing but creation. Yet again, Gilling was to be his source. He couldn't account for it, but somehow he only had to listen to Gilling and the words just seemed to flow. It had been like that right from the start.

It had begun quite unexpectedly, when his young brother Eric (now famous, under the name Justin Songbird, as manager of Masked Granny) had called round one evening. He had a problem. He had found the most terrible old woman in the world. She was so awful he daren't tell Potter the details – he might pass out. Eric was convinced that the woman could be a sensation, and, being Eric, he had her under a five-year contract. The trouble was, she wouldn't sing. He had given her fifteen different songs already, and she had loathed them all. She crumpled them into little balls and threw them at him. Sometimes she ate them.

Interesting, thought Potter, and idly dashed off a few whimsical lines. 'I'm so old, I'm falling to pieces . . .' Eric gasped, and rushed it to Masked Granny. The rest is history. Potter had gone from strength to strength as a songwriter, always making use of the same infallible technique. He simply sat and thought what Gilling would find most repulsive. Then he wrote it down.

Gilling was indispensable. He was the key to the whole thing. He was, so to speak, their barometer. Masked Granny was fascinated by Gilling. Will it offend Gilling, she would ask. If not, it must go. Chuckling evilly, she would listen to reports of Gilling's rapidly developing persecution complex, and devise means to aggravate it. And the more they fed Gilling's frenzy, the more Masked Granny's astounding success would escalate. Quite by accident, they had stumbled on the formula.

Potter looked at Gilling with a sort of tenderness. Poor Gilling, thrashing and foaming there on the floor. How could he ever have composed 'Senile Dementia' without Gilling's wounded sensibilities to guide him? And now he had it at last: the title of Masked Granny's next single. 'Foaming at the Mouth'. Potter drew out a blue notebook, and began, blissfully, to write.